D0167612

the
aztec
love
god

the aztec love god

tony diaz

NORMAL

Published by FC2
with support given by The English Department
Unit for Contemporary Literature of Illinois State University
and the Illinois Arts Council

Address all inquiries to:
FC2
Unit for Contemporary Literature
Campus Box 4241
Illinois State University
Normal, IL 61790-4241

ISBN: 1-57366-0361 (paperback)

Library of Congress Cataloging-in-Publication Data
Diaz, Tony.
The Aztec love god / Tony Diaz.— 1st ed.
p.   cm.
ISBN 1-57366-036-1 (alk. paper)
I. Title.
PS3554.12594a9   1998
813'.54—dc21   98-17585
                                                CIP

Book Design: Michele Steinbacher-Kemp
Cover Design: Todd Michael Bushman

Produced and Printed in the United States of America

Illinois ARTS Council
AN AGENCY OF THE STATE OF ILLINOIS

This program is partially sponsored by a grant from the Illinois Arts Council

Dedico todo mi trabajo a mi padre, Antonio Díaz, y a mi mamá, María Anita Díaz, quienes con su fe, amor, consejos, resos, trabajo, y respeto por la educación me inspiraron a tomar el camino mas difícil. Les debo todo. Gracias.

For my wife, Carolina, the woman of the dreams I did not know I could dream.

THE AZTEC LOVE GOD

I am a behind the scenes man. Invisible by choice, not unwillingly wiped off your central nervous system. No. Invisible to seep deeper into your receiving system, your super-central nervous system where the frequencies you experience but try to ignore make you nervous. There is where I plant the crops I pick.

[margin note: Invisibility = power]

But before I worked my way up to obscurity, I struggled insanely to attract the spotlight, to let it be known where I stood in the darkness, to show my spot in the universe. But the bright light always left me too eye-numb to see the floor, the faces of the shadows in front of me, and someone else always re-directed the light. *[margin note: keeping w/ what earlier Chicanos wanted to be]*

I was then a young, good Brown Man, tuned in only too well to the invisible messages floating through the mainstream; this current of events dictating which arm was my left arm, which arm was my right, and twisting one behind my back until I agreed.

Under this mental regime, I did not really know what The Aztec Love God was, though I had always suspected, though I have always been suspicious, and though I have always been suspect. Under this mental regime, I did not know what Sombrero *[margin note: stereotype]*

Hysteria was, though it festered in me. And I did not know that only T. A. L. G. could chase S. H. into the light—where it could pounce on it, get a clear picture of where to put its talons.

And only after The Aztec Love God knew his name could he name anything else. getting that power

Under this mental regime, I thought, like everyone else, that there were only two types of people on earth: You were either a willing participant of "The Real World" on MTV or a sucker on "Candid Camera." It was under that king that my energy was channeled into constructed ways, and my life slipped into a Mexican version of "Leave It to Beaver." "Leave It to Burro" my life could have been called, starring me, Tiofilio Duarte, as The Burro.

You see, my family *actually* lived in The Cleaver's old house.

In a fit of Sombrero Hysteria, years after the show went off the air, my dad cashed in the CD that was supposed to be my college fund and outbid other people for the house used for the set. Then he paid to have it moved to Chicago. Papa never mentioned college to me again, but I still had to help clean out all the beaver droppings from our new house. And it was my chore to every week paint over the graffiti on our white picket fence.

Every night, I prayed and prayed and prayed for the cancellation of "Leave It to Burro," until an episode just after my 17th birthday when I met my first girlfriend. Her name was Rosa Hernandez. Our families informed us that we were boyfriend and girlfriend during a banquet for the feast of La Virgen De Guadalupe. She was *muy caliente*—smooth-*West-Side-Story*-Rita-Moreno-caramel-pretty face with dark-*Heathers*-Winona-Ryder-obsidian-eyes. I tried to act as cool as I could while eating pastries shaped like the Virgin Mary. The second I bit into her halo, I had MTV visions of me and Rosa under a bingo table, her shaking my maracas. I said to her, in a cool Ricardo Montalban voice, "Let me take you out to dinner."

As a male, as my father's unwilling heir, I had a later curfew than Rosie which thereby extended her official leave. After dinner at The Olive Garden and a public screening of *La Bamba*, I used my extra hour and a half to get brave enough to put my arm around her. We kiss, then realize it's ten minutes to midnight, and my Chebby is about to turn into a pumpkin. The show closes with Mrs. Hernandez on the doorstep, welcoming me into the family, presenting me with a *Young Man's Bilingual Bible.*

One week later, Rosie and I make love behind a trucking warehouse. Real love. The most real love of its kind, with groping, fumbling, blushing. Real love, no body doubling, no black bars over body parts, no cosmetic surgery.

And REAL sex was not rated X!

There were more positions, more close-ups. Scents erupted. There was more than one point of contact, there were all those places where skin touched skin, all those points of contact, touch.

And there were all the plots leading into, through, and beyond the act.

It took a dick by the name of Jester to convince me to leave that love scene on the cutting room floor.

OPEN MIKE NITE

The first time I saw Jester was at an open mike night at Primo's, after I'd closed with an early version of The Aztec Love God. I was cleaning the whipped cream off the stage as the crowd was evaporating when I heard someone say, "Hey, Aztec, great set."

I looked over my shoulder and there was this six-foot-tall-bald-Caucasian-American in a dark blue sharkskin suit. He walked onto the stage.

"Thanks...guy." I almost called him Baldie.

"My brother's name is Guy, I'm Jester."

"My name's Tiofilio, but you can call me Tio." I'd heard of him. "Don't you manage those really tall skinny dudes?"

"That's right," he said. "'420 Pounds of Comedy,' three guys all over six feet tall but under 140 pounds. I also represent 'Three Bald Amazons' and my own act. I got a lot of projects goin' on. Which is what I want to talk to you about. Why don't we sit down? Someone else can take care of this mess."

I led him to where Rosie was sitting. All the lights had come on in the room, the place was emptying out, so there were only a few pockets of people closing their tabs. Last call had been a half hour ago, but Jester could still get service. He was a modern day Fonzie. Rosie looked shocked when I ordered a Bacardi and Coke. I cringed when she ordered only a soda. She was acting like such a minor.

"Listen, kid," Jester said. "I'm not gonna wait for my theme music to start or for the opening credits to stop rolling. Here's my program. I'm working on a project that can have you middlin' at Side Splitters, and getting paid, within two months. Does that sound good to you?"

"Hell yeah," I said, "that sounds good." Rosie smiled at me. "But who do I have to kill?" I asked.

"Yourself," Jester said. "You gotta give all this insane goofy-whipped-cream and jello shit a rest. You got good presence, good energy, now you need a focus, a persona."

"A whatta?"

"Exactly," Rosie piped up. "That's what I was trying to tell you the other night, but you got mad."

I gave her the eye.

"Listen, T-O, for this new troupe I'm putting together, I got an Oriental named Hon Cho, who's here tonight, and a Black guy who calls himself Ram Bo. I need one more man."

"Oh, shit," I said. "Listen, here's a word from my sponsor. No. That Paul Rodriguez, Cheech and Chong stuff's played out. I'm up to something new, cutting edge."

"Kid, you think you're doing something completely new, but I've seen other comics do the same bits you're doing."

"I haven't stolen shit."

"I just mean you don't own it."

Rosie jumped in. "Anyway, Tio, that's not the kind of SELL-OUT show you've had in mind."

Jester turned and looked around, like he was gonna offer the gig to one of the people left in the club.

"I want you to talk to someone," Jester said. He yelled, "Hey, Hon Cho," across the room to an Asian guy in a gray striped suit. He was flirting with three waitresses. They were all laughing, staring at him like he was a TV Guide and they were hungry viewers. Jester kept calling his name. Besides the help, now there were only these two comedians, us, and a guy and a lady at a table, arguing with the manager about the bill.

A bartender finally yelled, "For God's sake Hon Cho, an-swer Jester. These ladies gotta help clean up."

Hon Cho stomped over. I looked at his feet for hooves. He

was wearing these bad ass snake skin boots. "This better be good, Tall-Bald-and-Ugly," he said to Jester.

"T-O, this is Hon Cho, The Eastern Cowboy."

"Howdy," he said. He had really smooth hands, but a firm handshake. What I always remember about Hon Cho was his hair. It was so styled it looked fake. It was blue-black and combed over to the side to give it a wave, but he must have spent hours applying just the right amount of cement to each strand and holding it in place until it hardened. Eventually I'd catch him on stage, jumping around, claiming that even after an earthquake he would still look good.

"Hon Cho," Jester pulled him into the chair next to him and put his arm around him, "T-O here thinks that by asking him to make the most of his ethnicity, I'm asking him to sell out or something."

"Oh no, pardner," Hon Cho said. "That's not the case, T-O. By not doing anything with your ethnicity, it's like you're this three-hundred-pound-guy trying to use regular pick up lines to make it with the ladies. You say, 'Hey, Babe, what's your sign?' She says, 'Two ton limit, fat boy.'

"Unless you bring up the weight first, the audience hears your act and thinks, 'Here's this fat guy standing there telling me jokes about this or that.' They might laugh, but they're always thinking, 'Man, this guy is fat.'"

Rosie said, "That's stupid."

"How much of my act did you guys actually catch?"

Jester said he caught most of it. "I liked that updating the classics of literature bit. 'I turned MacBeth into M C Beth.' I liked that. But that had nothing to do with the rest of your act."

A waitress gave Jester a bill and said that we really had to leave now. "This one's on me, T. Maybe I'll see you around some time." Jester stood, stuck his hand into a pocket inside the sharkskin suit, whipped out a fifty, dropped it on the bill and turned to leave.

"Wait up." I pictured myself turning 21 and still writing twenty jokes a day for free. "You've got Ram Bo. You've got Hon Cho. I guess that would make me Burr-o."

"That's got possibilities, kid." He turned around and threw his arms open. "Here's my card. Call me tomorrow."

Rosie gave me the silent treatment in the car. As I drove, she opened her purse and pulled out her lipstick, eye shadow, eyeliner and stuck the stuff in my glove compartment. I drove to our trucking warehouse. She pulled out her compact and started wiping her face with cotton swabs. She checked herself in the small mirror, moved it round and round, trying to fit in it, checking to make sure she was clean. She tossed the cotton balls out of the window so that there was no way humanly possible that her parents could find out she'd been wearing makeup.

Kissing her cheek, I could smell the club in Rosie's hair, cigarette smoke mixed with the imitation-Obsession I'd bought her (Addiction it was called), mixed with the smell of our leather jackets. I loved the sound of our jackets rubbing. She pulled away and pointed at her watch. I dropped her off, then drove home by myself, braying out the car window.

THE RESISTANCE

But before I could invest the time in selling out, I had to first buy in. That was the purpose of Honors Religion IV. Honors Religion at 8:10 a.m. Honors Religion IV meant that the next morning was a weak day mourning, and I was institutionalized in an all-male Catholic high school run by the Basillian Brothers. I'd picked the school like I now pick settings for TV shows: far enough from home so that I won't bump into anyone I know. Close enough to home so that I know how things work. And in order to tolerate the sunlight, the imposed order, the cafeteria food, I sent another me in my place.

My parents didn't speak English well, so I'd been writing my own absentee notes and signing my report cards since grammar school. I also knew of lots of people who'd bought, used, forged or stolen papers to create new identities—overnight. So with the Basillian Brothers, I registered, took the entrance exam and signed all my papers "Antonio Marquez." I'd seen the name in the credits for a Spanish soap opera and thought it sounded cool: "Antonio"—ethnic and sophisticated, "Tony" when I'm being casual. And "Marquez" as in Spanish for "marquis," French for "royalty," and it sounded like "sign" in English.

capitalist dream

It was "Antonio Marquez" who I sent to De La Salle Institute. He was smart and funny, but not trying to go pro. Not unless he caught a big break or made some money at it was he going to reveal to the fellas what he did at night instead of hanging-out with them. And 5 hours of sleep had made him realize that Jester's offer would not impress the Mexican-American Leadership Organization or MALO. (If we had been born and cultivated on the other side, perhaps our name would have been *Buenos Alumnos Dedicados* or BAD.)

To the administration, MALO was simply another student organization. But we were really an underground, Hyper Ultra-Affirmative Action Program. Our covert mission statement read: "MALO is a chance for us to learn how to form our own secret societies, our own monopolies, our own networks. It's the chance for us to corporatize what we have so far only been able to accomplish with gangs, sets, crews. So that when THEY take Affirmative Action away, we will be able to take care of ourselves, each other."

We wrote essays for students, memorized, wrote out then sold test questions (answers were extra). We forged absentee notes. I even took the ACT for two guys. We were regular intellectual terrorists. Young American businessmen in the making.

At the top of my comedy notebook, which was the closest that I would get to a diary, for that day I'd written "THE MORE YOU KNOW THE MORE YOU CAN MAKE FUN OF."

Channel 0

0755-0850 **Honors** Religion IV.
Accelerated knowledge of God. The extra five commandments (50% MORE). Three fabulous new beatitudes and a sacrament. And no, this will not be on the ACT.

0855-0910 Homeroom Denouncements
The Hour Father. The Pledge of a Lesion.

0915-1010 Honors Chemistry
Today's question: "What does the periodic table become when it's not a table?"
The beginning of a joke about James "covalent" Bond—interrupted by the door creaking open. ("The door creaked open..." was what I wrote, "and it creaked intentionally, like

the creaker was fiddling with the creak spot, milking it for all it's worth.") And then the smell of smoke, maybe gunfire debris, witch burnings, book burnings, or unfiltered cigarrettes. Mr. Wallace Autruck, the principal, stepped into the class. All of us, including the teacher, turned to look at him. Even though Autruck dressed like a principal, his hair was just messy enough, there was always a scuff on his shoes or a thread steaming out from his tie that let you know he was on the edge, two suits away from life on the lam. And he was staring at me.

"Marquez, come with me."

I'd been expecting this for a week. I picked up my books in one swoop and sauntered to the door. I counted the beats and measured the length of my stride. It was imperative that I walk as if I was sure that it would be only a rerun of the If-you-disrupt-the-ACT-Inquisition-you-will-be-EX-communicated routine. I could not walk as if I feared expulsion, because I did. This spotlight would be an interrogation light.

To prepare for this moment, I'd removed all guilty thoughts from my mind, hid under the folds of my brain what I suspected he might suspect, left only pure ideas for him to yell at.

Away from the safety of the monotony of the seats with the unmovable desks and hurled into Wally's World with his bulletin board of secret messages, all sorts of printouts with just numbers, all numbers (and during my four years there we stole sheet after sheet off that board, had genius after genius study it, but we never figured out what the hell the code was or if Wally was just fucking with us with that bulletin board, which, of course, would have meant he was a genius. I preferred to think he was stupid enough to memorize some bizarre code so he could keep track of how often each of us farted or cursed).

"This is not *Stand and Deliver*, or 'Room 204,' and I am not 'Welcome Back Kotter,' so don't act like a sweathog with me, Marquez," Mr. Autruck yelled. I practiced my right to remain silent. "I am going to ask you one question and I want you to answer it right away. No pausing. Do you understand?"

"Was that the question?" I let wussiness seep into my voice, but I refused to admit to myself that I was scared.

"Are you trying to be a comedian, Marquez?" Mr. Autruck threatened me with his size XXXL green suit coat from Bob's Big Boy Shoppe, squeaking his Payless-plastic-wing-tip shoes at me, shoving that wide-brown-knit-K-Mart tie in my face, the smell of burnt heretics. "Answer me, Marquez. Are you trying to be a comedian?" He said this to me and because I couldn't change his channel, I bit my tongue. "No, your Impotence," I muttered.

"Now this is the question. Answer right away. Okay?"

I nodded my head. I had to pay careful attention to the exact way he would phrase this next thing.

"Did you or have you ever taken a test?"

"Of course I've taken a test." And I scrunched my face at the question to make him feel insecure about the thing.

"Listen carefully," he said, staring me right in the eye. "When I say 'take,' Marquez, I mean steal. Did you steal a test?"

"What?"

"Quick, answer."

"No. I didn't steal any test." And I made like I was gonna stand because of the nerve of his question.

"Sit down. The word in the halls is that you and your ya-hoos are the punks who stole Mr. Ravetti's test."

"We didn't steal any test. I swear."

"How do you know they were stolen?"

"You just told me."

"Did I? I don't remember TELLING you anything."

"I need a lawyer."

"Don't get wise." He stood over me with his hands on his hips as if to show me how to stand straight but to not dare to stand. "I have a student who is ready to finger everyone involved."

"I don't wanna be fingered."

"What?"

"I mean, I didn't do anything wrong." It's a balancing act. I have to act indignant, yet scared, yet not guilty-scared.

"Even if I don't bust you, Marquez, you better realize that to get into any good college, you'll need recommendations from your teachers. And 'Attitude' and 'Cooperation' are on every rec. I've ever seen. And if I find out later that you knew who was mixed up in this—you will pay."

"I know, I know I have to submit, submit my applications." Autruck thinks I'm so scared I might piss my pants. "May I please go to the lavatory?" I ask. After four years, you figure out a guy's timing, and this is exactly when he would let me breathe, er...piss.

I ran into a stall, whipped out a pen, ripped some toilet

paper off the roll and wrote: "Before Waldo became a principal at an all-male Catholic high school he was a hooker in the Philippines who got rich by undercutting everyone else's prices and mastering the use of every limb for sex until she raised enough money for a ticket to the states, a sex change, plenty of steroids and souvenirs for the family that abandoned her in the wilds of Newark where a garbage barge man picked her up and shipped her off to Bombay with a load of garbage from her family's house, and all she had left was a late bill from the phone company with her folks' number and address and bill amount, and even though they abandoned her she still bought them presents before her trip back to the States for the sex-change operation (we do after all have some of the best surgeons out here), but she splurged so much she only had enough money left to buy a very small penis. And then he became the principal of an all-male Catholic high school."

It wasn't exactly a joke, but it made me feel better in a voodoo kind of way. And it was joke number six for the twenty that day, for the 140 that week, for the 640 that month, for the 33,280 that year. And compared to that number, Wally didn't seem so tough. I looped the toilet paper around my hand; it made me look like a boxer wearing wraps.

When I stepped into the hall, my head felt as if I'd been sucking helium, tugging right then left all of sudden. I walked slowly to wear off the wooze, ran my hand along the wall for help.

For over a week I'd expected this little meeting, played out scenarios in my head, but it's never like the real thing, no matter how well you prepare.

Of course I hadn't stolen the test.

I never stole tests. Never "stole" a test as in I never stuck a piece of paper in a lock so that it would not lock when the door closed and then sneaked in to the classroom and went through the teacher's desk, found the exams and took one. No.

My specialty was memorizing every question on a test and then writing them down after class. A new recruit brainstormed the Ravetti Heist, conned us into helping plan this display of brute strength, and pulled off the job two weeks earlier.

This kid, "lower case k" let's call him, was part of our new class of recruits, and he had the same problem they all had. Either they were too smart and not tough enough, or too tough and not smart enough. "k" was tough. He and his cohorts sold too many tests, so too many morons earned "A's."

When we started asking "k" questions about the job, his left eye started twitching, he started sweating like a cartoon. He couldn't remember how sloppy he'd been when he lifted the test, he couldn't remember what had happened to the original. It took me two days to track down and destroy it.

Before walking back into class I forced my head straight and recalculated a saunter.

If I acted scared after coming back from the office, most of our customers would have confessed to any crime or travesty put before them. The best policy was sitting down and hitting the books. I was scared, but I couldn't let anyone, even myself, know I was scared. I had to appear to the teacher as if I was taking notes, and I had to appear to the students as if I was fooling the teacher by doodling instead.

1015-1110 Honors Physics
Guest Rapper "MC Squared" explains how the only constants in the universe are the speed of light, the suckiness of life, and pains in your ass. The cosmos will always be screwing you over. And all three combine to creat the Theory of Everything. You will be tested on this every day of your life.

1115-1215 Lunch/Intramurals
Eat shit and die.

LUNCH TIME, LUNCH TIME, means it's time for CHANNEL 99—The Underground Network's presentation of MONTY ZUMA'S HEROES.

I called an emergency meeting of MALO. We'd been meeting every day since we realized so many intellectually-challenged students (morons) earned "A's" on Ravetti's test. "Emergency meeting" simply meant everyone was required to attend.

I met first with the other MALO leaders, "A" and "B." Since the beginning of MALO, we'd expected something like this, so we created different checks and balances to cover our asses. First off, we all went by a letter instead of a full name. I was the fourth guy in the group, the last of the founders, so I was called "D," the last of the upper-case letters. "A" is now a senator and "B" is a big-time lawyer. Neither of them will have anything to do with me now. So they appear in silhouette with their voices disguised.

"C" started school with us but graduated early. He was the visionary, the heart and brain behind the beginning of the group, author of the public mission statement and the covert mission statement. He went off to college and a few years later got killed in a riot on campus, a riot he started. "A" and "B" distanced themselves from that too.

"I don't know you two, mutherfuckers," "A" (the future senator) said, "When this shit hits the fans, I don't know you two mutherfuckers."

Me and "B" laughed because he was serious, and we had never seen him piss his pants like this.

"Relax," "B" (the future lawyer) told him. "No one's got shit on us. None of us has sold a test ourselves in three years. None of us has sold an essay or done anything that can be used as direct evidence against us. And if anyone who's used a MALO test tries to turn on us, we've got receipts with their names on them for whatever they've bought."

"Right!" "A" cheered up. "If things get bad, all we need to do is leak those receipts."

"I don't think we have to worry about anyone from the outside fuckin' us over," I said.

"That's right," "A" added, "the new guys fucked up. They're the ones who'll fuck us over, on mistake."

"They're morons," the senator called them. "The worst kind of Hispanic you can dream up: simple, unambitious, dumb."

"Relax," I shouted, "We got them into this."

They both stared at me.

"Don't worry. I can calm them down," I told them. "I've got 'Silent-e' rounding them all up. A few were scared to show up to today's meeting, but he's good. He'll get them all here. And I'll talk to them. If we can calm them down, assure them that everything will work out, then everything WILL work out."

"I want to talk to them first," senator "A" said. I figured we could try the good cop, bad cop routine. "Sure," I said. "You go first, then I'll finish up."

The first member walked in; it was time to establish the room. I like to let the crowd see me ignore them as it files in; it must know that they are in MY space. Here I was the connection, I helped disperse the "big breaks."

I met the dress code in the clothes I'd haggled for on Maxwell Street: twenty-dollar silver sheen baggy pants, a twenty-dollar gray athletic-cut shirt with a white collar (came with a gold pin to run through the collar buttons, for when I need to look Real Down), a skinny, black tie I resurrected from my dad's Zoot Suiter closet, and I had on the leather armor—The Jacket: twenty pounds of leather, wide shoulders, three inside pockets. And I was standing in Stacy Adam's black shoes with a white band gliding across 'em, pointy enough to kill the cockroaches in the corner.

My associates were similarly dressed, though I have to admit that the senator's shoes were the pointiest and his tie the skinniest; it was almost a string.

The last soldier in closed the door behind him.

"Well, the only person missing is 'k'," said the Senator. Because we were selective, and because not every Latino student wanted to be in MALO, we'd gotten only to lower-case "l" in the alphabet. There were 10 guys crowded into the room.

No one dared ask where "k" might be. If Silent-e could not find him, he was either absent or in Wally's clutches.

"Who brought 'k' in?" the Senator asked, but we already knew the answer. He was just saying out loud what everyone was thinking. We all looked at "j."

"Listen, bro. Ese muchacho es tight-lipped," "j" squirmed. "He won't lingo."

"I knew we shouldn't've let a Puerto Rican in," said an insignificant consonant.

"Let's not get into that again," "B" said. "We can't exclude anyone because he's not Mexican. That would be racist. Besides, he's still Hispanic."

"Like 'C' used to say though," the senator was practicing his rabble rousing, "we're united only by the conquest."

But it was not yet time for rousing. "Muchachos, relax," I said. "Ol' boy ain't squealed yet. We trained him right. And if he turns out to be a bitch, er...I mean a snitch, he's the only leak we have. He can talk all he wants. If we maintain a tight circle, he'll look like a liar." There was a murmur of assent, approving crowd noise. Then a knock at the door.

We froze.

I gave a signal. Everyone pulled out and started to concentrate on "projects, minutes, important files" we had set up. They checked each other for stolen answer keys, test pages, guilty looks, receipts for term papers as I walked to the door, raised the posterboard touting our name and peeked through the window. It was Esperanzo, office slave for the day, and one of the chief Latinos who not only did not want to join MALO, but had been directly quoted as saying he would like to see the end of us. This kid had gone to De La Salle instead of Quigley South, the seminary school, because he WANTED to become a priest, but the seminary's curriculum was not as rigorous. This was another direct quote.

I lowered the sign, unlocked the door and let him in.

"Marquez," he stepped in, "hello." He had a bunch of slips in his hand.

"Esperanzo, hello."

He spoke in a whisper, even though everyone else was acting occupied. "I have bad news. Autruck's having a shit fit." He paused. I'd never heard him swear. He looked me right in the eye. "I know you and I do not see things eye to eye, Marquez, but I want you to know that that doesn't mean I want to witness your demise." I did not know what to say. "Mr. Autruck could have sent any other orderly with these notes, but he waited for me. I think he wanted to send you some kind of message by having *me* deliver these. Well, I have my own message which is this: We both have very different ways of getting there, but I think we both agree on the same end. And you should know that they are both very hard roads."

I was stunned. I could only shake my head. "Thank you," I know I said. "Thank you."

Esperanzo held up the wad of papers in his hand. "Mr. Autruck has sent love notes for each of you to go to the office, fifteen minutes apart." He handed them to me.

I took the notes, and he left.

Wally also wanted to let us know that he knew we were meeting, and he knew who was in our group.

I told the fellows what the sheets were.

I could see a few of the consonants get a little queasy. I've seen it on stage, someone who doesn't have his act together, still memorizing lines, not sure if they're funny or he's funny, this someone gets a few mean looks from the crowd and prophecies a bad set, is already struggling with bombing, getting over that pale feeling. It takes a lot of strength just not to cry. And this was even before I passed out the notes, one for each of them, each with an exact time written on it. Fifteen minutes was about ten minutes more than an average student, one who wasn't trained or practiced, this was ten minutes more than most guys could stand.

"*Paz*," I told them. "I want everyone to have a seat. 'B' is gonna say a little something and then I will." A lower-case letter moved to the floor so that I could have a chair.

"B" began to pontificate.

"Deny everything. If they show you a picture of you selling the answers to a test, claim that it's not you." He was talking fast, and straining to make eye contact with everyone. Just enough to convey an appalling sense of desperation. "If they accuse you of something, don't give in. Don't ever confess, no matter what. Get your parents to believe you. Get them to come to school. If your parents won't come, we'll get you parents who will.

"Remember that you are innocent. Tell yourself this so many times that when you go to sleep you dream about your innocence.

"As long as you keep your mouth shut, nothing will go wrong." Most of the fellows avoided his gaze.

"I plan to go to Harvard next year. Harvard began recruiting me when I was a junior. If we get through this, I can promise you that they will start recruiting you when you're a junior, too. But you have to have a friend there first. I'm that friend. I will be your Affirmative Action Program. You will be my legacy, I will be your connection. If you're my friend, you will remain honest. You will let THEM know you are honest. You will say you have done nothing wrong. None of MY friends is a crook."

The second his lips stopped moving, he sat down.

I've never had a crowd as unnerved by an opening act. He eliminated any chance I had of speaking to the group rationally. I had to rise above logic.

To show them that I didn't care who heard, I said nice and loud, "Autruck doesn't have shit on us.

"If he really knew what was goin' down, parents would've been called, expulsion papers or at least detentions would've been produced, heads would be rolling, not office-slaves delivering notes." I walked around the room to see how that was sinking in. And the color was coming back to some of them.

"When I was in eighth grade, some kids were stealing Mrs. Rently's raffle money. She kept it in this plastic jack-o-lantern on her desk, and well, let's just say some kids weren't delivered from temptation." This got a few empathetic giggles. "One day she figured out that money was missing and decided to drop the axe. Now pretty much the whole class knew which four or five kids were into this. I have to admit I was not. I was busy running an underground lottery game. I didn't need or want her thirty-five cents. As a matter of fact, I think a few kids stole from Mrs. Rently to pay me." I took the laugh. And I have to admit it was a perfect time for a little levity, a perfect time to assert that I was not a common criminal and THUS they weren't either. "But what Mrs. Rently did was say to the whole room that she knew exactly who it was and she was going to give them one chance to turn themselves in. She said she was gonna step out of the room, go down the hall, and when she came back she wanted the person to step forward or to leave a note on her desk. And if they turned themselves in, they would be in less trouble. But if they didn't, they would be in a whole 'hell' of a lot of trouble—and she said 'hell' so we would all think she meant trouble—and anyone who knew about it would get catch hell, too. Stealing and lying are serious sins, she said.

"I could just about feel the whole eighth grade blush, and I could see some of the kids look toward the kids who were in on it, which if Rently was smart should've been enough. She could've figured out who was stealing by who everyone stared at and who I avoided looking at. I was still rough around the edges back then."

"Uh, 'D'," this came from a very lower case un-consonant. "But shouldn't we be getting ready to go? It's almost time for the first meeting and..."

"No, no, no. We need to relax, keep cool, not scurry."

The senator added, "They don't have us where they want us. We need to put them where we want them."

I still don't know what the hell that meant but I said, "Exactly! The important thing to know is that these four kids didn't step up. Who did step up was a kid named Stephen Patrakus who we all knew didn't have anything to do with the whole thing. But he was hunched over his desk, scribbling and then ripped a small strip of paper out of a notebook, stepped up and left the sheet on her desk. So we all knew he was snitching. And after he sat down we could hear Mrs. Rently down the hall talking to the 7th grade teacher, talking loud so we could hear that she meant business.

"I just didn't think the whole thing was right. And me and Steve didn't get along, so I figured he might be trying to frame me, too. So I ran up and grabbed the paper off her desk, and the second after I sat down Mrs. Rently stepped back in."

The bell sounded and the first of our letters had five minutes to get to his meeting with Wally, and the rest of us them had five minutes to get to class and sweat until his time.

"The punk tried to tell on me, that he had put a paper on the desk and someone took it, which got Rently pissed. Then she asked him who took it. So not only had he tried to snitch once, I now had the proof in my desk, and he was about to snitch a second time.

"And then one of the thieves called him a liar. And then another thief called him a liar, and then another. And Rently had a look on her face like the number of kids in her room had just doubled. And then it gets all loud. And I know Steve has got to be thinking that he's gonna get his ass kicked real bad, first by these four kids and then worse by me.

"So he confesses to stealing the money! He even says that he made the shit up about the paper on the desk, that he was trying to get out of trouble, that he meant to put something on the desk but she came back too soon.

"Well, all of sudden I felt bad for the kid. But what I couldn't do was check to see who was on the list 'cause during all the accusations and shouting, I fuckin' swallowed the piece of paper. I figured if she got to searching me and found the paper on me, I was dead, so I ate it. And it probably took me a while to shit and piss out who he narc-ed on. He might have been exact, he might have put me on the list, he might have had the whole damn room on there or maybe he just had *his* name on there. Maybe he knew he was hated and wanted to make it up to us, and maybe I fucked everything up. The poor guy was too busy sobbing to explain it to Rently, and I'm sure she could not have been able to understand. All I know is she took the kid to the office, and we never saw him again. And this was all because this kid thought Rently knew as much as she threatened to know."

They all looked at me as if I had huge wings, their eyes wide, them smiling too much, wanting to look me in the eye, some laughing a little, giddy with glee.

"Now this is high school, so their techniques are more sophisticated. And they'll get tougher in college, then graduate school, and they're absolutely diabolical in the business world, but by then we've figured out their games because we've passed tests like this. All we have to do is stick together."

Someone asked, "What if they try to disband MALO?"

"They'll have to be sly," I assured him. "If they handle it the wrong way, we can go to the news with this."

The lawyer caught the fever. "Shit, if 'C' was here he'd be beggin' for that to happen. We'd probably have a lawsuit on our hands."

"Do you think Esperanzo told on us? Is he this Steve Patrakas?" The room got dead quiet. I forget who asked this question. It might have even been my subconsicous throwing its voice into the mouths of a small letter. "No, my friend." And there is a certain way that you have to phrase things for some people. "You see,...." And it takes a lot of work and time to figure out a new and complex answer. "Esperanzo is brown." But it is very easy to answer in an established line of thought, a soundbite. "Steve was white.

"The point of the story is that we must all stick together." I heard affirmatives in the background, high-fives. So it seemed we were all united.

I felt spent, all that energy forcing those huge wings out of my back. But I could see that this had really helped them. They each patted me on the back as I handed them the little slips from Wally with their names on it, one for everyone of them except me, "k," and "C."

We went to class.

Channel 0 resumes overly-broad casting.

1220-1315 Honors American History III
                    Civil War Reruns
1320-1415 Honors British Lit.
                    Early Shakespearean Sitcoms

Waiting for either the Vatican Army to bust through the door or the bell to ring, I updated more classics of literature from my desk in the corner:

I turned *All Quiet on the Western Front* into *All Chillin' on da' West Side*.

I turned the *Scarlet Letter* into *The Day-Glo Letter*.

I turned *Lord of the Flies* into *Lord of the Fly Girls*.

At 2:10 into the parking lot pulled a yellow Buick filled with girls tightly wrapped in the yellow blouses of Maria High School. I zoomed into the sunlight bouncing off Rosie's coffee-cream legs as she stepped out of the car, her butt as she leaned in to say bye to her friends, and I said bye to the silent treatment I'd expected.

The banana yellow Buick with the creamy filling pulled away. And I was a little closer to getting away from this place for a few hours, another day closer to graduation, to my name on a marquee.

There was a pretty girl in a leather jacket leaning on my car, waiting for me to get out of school. "Yeah," I thought to myself. "I can kick the shit out of Fonzie."

And then the hunchback of Notre Dame started chiming the school bell, clanging it as we were released into the atmosphere.

Rosie kissed me in the parking lot. She must've been feeling a little like Madonna. My fellow Catholics hooted, beeped as they stormed out. I scanned the area for my MALO friends. "Did you hurt your hand?" She noticed the toilet paper.

"No, that's just some homework." "A" and "B" passed in "B's" car and gave me the signal. They were smiling.

"Well, I have a present for you." She handed me a round package wrapped in brown paper. The paper was thick, with crisscrossed tape. She laughed while I fumbled with it. "Come on," she said. "It's not like it's a bra." All of a sudden I was feeling a little like Ricky Ricardo. I heard another beep and got the signal again.

The first peek I got of the gift was a patch of white fur, then a black dot, more fur, another dot. She'd given me a pair of fuzzy dice. "Thanks for the dead white mice," I said.

"Four jour Chebby," she said.

"I get it. I get it." She had a way of making me think that the last important thing that happened to her was the last thing she did with me.

She threw her weight against me, arms around my neck, pinned me to the car. "Listen, m'ijo, I'm sorry about saying 'I told you so' in front of Jester last night."

Another car passed and I got the beep, the signal, and smiles from two more of my boys.

"That's okay, sweetheart. Believe me, after today, I miss last night. I could keep living it over and over."

"And I'm sorry about speaking my mind."

"Uh...that's okay."

"And I'm sorry for not walking three paces behind you."

"You always apologize for that but you always forget."

"And I want you to know that I'm proud of you for getting so good so fast at everything you set your mind too. And I mean everything...." She raised and lowered her eyebrows. She was amazing. And behind her I could see Wally Autruck step alone out of his building and stand in front of his doors with his arms crossed.

"Jester's right. You're good. But he's wrong about the Mexican stuff." She tilted my head back and stuck her tongue down my throat.

"Wow!" I gently got her arms off me and stood straight. "Tell you what, Sweetie. Let's not worry about him right now. I'm not changing anything for anyone. I don't want anything to do with him. All I want to think about is graduating and getting out of here."

I took her by the hand to the passenger side door and let her into my car. I ran around to my side without turning, but I still felt Wally's stare as if he was sitting on my back. I took off my jacket, tossed it in my back seat, jumped in and flipped the ignition.

I didn't just throw my right arm around Rosie, I loved touching her. I loved as many points of contact as possible. I rolled my shirt sleeves up so I could feel the exposed part of her neck along my bicep and the crook of my elbow; her hair fell on the back of my arm; my forearm and hand pressed against the side of her upper shoulder, pulling her closer to my warm ribs, my chest. She folded her legs underneath herself, leaving her shiny, cinnamon-colored knees peeking out from under her skirt, kneading into my leg.

I deftly shifted and steered with my left hand after so much practice. She had her hand on my thigh, and I let her play with the knobs of my stereo, turning up the bass on my 14-inch Jensen speakers, pushing in my cassette of hot mixes, music with hundreds upon hundreds of beats per minute, street music with sampling—a nice word for stealing phrases, lyrics, and chords from other songs, commercials, TV—and scratching—ruining records 'cause it sounded great. We drove off to the producers of the "Leave It to Burro Show," broadcasting at 30 decibels the thump, thump, thump of my big boom-box heart.

A BRIEF HISTORY OF
MEXICAN-AMERICAN TIME

Though everyone agrees that it is 1996, what most people don't realize is that some people weren't introduced to this way of keeping time until 1519, when the Aztecs took Cortez's very, very strict catechism class. Before then, the Aztecs used a different calendar. So 1519 to them was the year of 7 reed, 6 cactus, and 1 Chihuahua. However, their calendar had several drawbacks. First of all, it was circular and made out of stone, tough to lug around on a long commute.

The Aztecs also believed the world had been destroyed four times previously and a fifth time was coming, so there were several days on the calendar when temple priests sacrificed people in order to stave off the fifth destruction of the world. If you were one of the people sacrificed, obviously you might not care what happened to the world. But the temple priests thought they were doing you an honor by relieving you of all your VISA bills and letting you save the world at the same time. I can almost hear them say, "This is going to hurt me more than it hurts you." In Aztec of course.

Some Aztecs quickly embraced Cortez's Catholic calendar. It was lighter and had a picture of a horse for each month.

The Spaniards also strongly discouraged the letting of blood—unless it was to encourage a heathen to listen to them.

Devils, miracles, holy ghosts, Spring Break. Yes, some Aztecs loved the new calendar.

But there was a tough transition period.

After all, the Spanish had had 1,500 years to catch on to this mode of keeping time. The Aztecs, one day to the next, had to change all their stationery, all their checks. They had to fling all those stone calendars out the window. Well, actually fling them off the pyramid altars. And all their checks just said _____ Reed. Now they would have to say 15___. If it had to happen, at least it didn't happen 21 years or so earlier. Then Aztecs would've had to have checks printed up that said 14___, and then boom, the next century comes, and they'd have to change them again. Quite an expense.

So for a while, the Spaniards and Aztecs were on different time. To the Spaniards it was 1,521-years-after-Christ-was died. To the Aztecs it was 2-years-after-these-soldiers-of-Christ-kicked-our-collective-butt.

The whole Christmas concept wasn't clear to them either.

One historian uncovered the following letter to the editor in one of the first New World newspapers, the *Mexico City Bugle*.

"One minute you dirty Spaniards are trying to kill us, and today, the year of 8 reed, I mean December 25th, two-years-after-Christ-kicked-our-butts, you're giving us fruitcakes? Why?"

This actually incited a few rebellions when old warriors thought the Spanish were trying to poison them. A grievance filed with the Vatican reads, "Look I survived the smallpox, the branding, but this garbage..."

But leap year, this they could understand.

Crumbs from each day stolen, hidden here and there. And this builds up and builds up, even though you don't notice. And then boom, time that you thought was lost or wasted, that time was actually stolen and is being used to throw your schedule out of whack—if you're not careful.

The Aztecs understood this and thought, in Aztec of course, "The world was destroyed five times this way, just wait.

"You might think this is 1,523 years after the birth of Christ, but to us it's four-years-after-the-world-was-destroyed-a-fifth-time.

"We're just hanging around for the sixth world. And the sixth time's the charm. Merry Easter."

CASA SANCHEZ

Hot vapor enveloped us when I shoved open the front door. My mom was boiling beans in the kitchen, and we would boil with them. I slammed the door twice to get it to close. Because of the house's crooked frame, the door did not fit just right. My folks most likely barely noticed the slam because it was a regular occurrence and because the television blared a Spanish dubbed commerical for underarm spray. *Sobacos* means "arm pits" in Spanish. On entering, there was a painting of Jesus bleeding as he prayed in the garden of Gethsemane. Under it, roses from my mother's garden; a wooden rosary holder with short protruding sticks high enough to let dangle the blue, red, white, silver beaded strings and crosses, each an abacus of prayers, a strung out prayer wheel, dried string beans with the knuckles protruding through the skin worn away from so many syllables aimed at Heaven. My mom always prayed just as hard as He did in the garden but would never insult Him by out-bleeding Him.

I never brought outsiders home.

Besides the fact that I knew we would seem strange to most anyone, on top of that, one side of the house had different colored walls, different size windows, and did not perfectly connect with the rest of the house. It felt odd more than looked strange right away.

Cliché, familiar enough looked the hall, the living room, and the room designated for the preparation of food to consume. And inside this kitchen sat this device which caught airwaves and translated them into moving images, like a phone taking constant one-way calls, describing, dressing, telling us what the wave after wave of messages travelling through the air, passing right through us, not under our nose, through our heads, through our milking cows, washing over our cars, spraying traffic, coursing through the city, over the skyscrapers, what wave after wave after wave was saying. The TV in the kitchen pulled in the images of "Telemundo"—a new Spanish soap opera, previews for MTV Internacional, Spanish beer-commercials starring Spuds Mackenzie, the beer guzzling pooch (which was why Bud Light tasted like dog piss).

Father, home early from his imaginary job, dissected jalapeños under the glow of "Telemundo" while Mom stirred the beans. Bright red sides of skirt steak lay on the table, outlined in dull white fat. "Goo afterr nooon," my mom said, smiling, exaggerating her accent. That was her best bit, flinging English words at us when we didn't expect it. Then my father shocked me by greeting me. "*Buenas tardes*, Junior." When he was home at what he considered an "unmanly" hour (many soap operas on TV was a good indication of the femininity of a particular hour), he did not like to acknowledge my existence which would thereby acknowledge his own existence. I kinda nodded my head at him, scared he had watched some talk show on parenting, wondering if he would try to hug me, or ask me how my day went.

Rosie tossed her jacket on the couch in the living room, walked into the killing room to the refrigerator and pulled out lemons. She grabbed a knife from the sink and quartered the lemons. She rubbed them on the raw meat. My parents smiled. I think they both came. "Eskoot ober," Mom said to Dad, and Rosie moved between them. I get a nice long shot of them together at the table, the new Cleavers, just a regular Fuck'n family.

I sauntered through the swinging door (It was my favorite door because it worked fine.) and into the living room and grabbed the newspaper to search for topical jokes hidden between the headlines. I needed to write six more jokes for my twenty for that day, but it was so damn hot from the boiling beans that I felt as if I was having lemons rubbed on ME.

I plopped down on our leather couch, unwrapped the toilet paper on my hand, and switched my brain to three track, mixing the conversation between my producers and Rosie; the musical transitions and the screams of the telenovela; and the headlines, story previews, sub-headlines, blurb boxes, ads, pictures.

"You know, Rosie," my dad said. "I learneda English froma the television. My verbal skills havea dramatically increased by 30%–almost over night." Rosie laughed while I read about a televangelist who'd been caught with a hooker, accepting a donation in-kind, the congregation would get their cut later. "Rosie," Mom said in Spanish with the English subtitles I think in, "can you please put these potatoes in *el pica le i pica le,*" the poke-it-here-and-poke-it-there. Most mothers would just say "nuke this for me" if they were feeling nutty. But the scary part is that Rosie knew what Mom meant. She stuck the potatoes in the microwave for 10 minutes while a prisoner on death row sued the state for not providing him with a color TV. Maybe he'll settle out of court if said televangelist takes his confession and hears his last prayer. I stared at the women modeling bras in the ads under a story about the rising, skyrocketing, boner of inflation. And the musical crescendo accented the realization of the wealthy family's most arrogant son—he was given birth by the maid! Poor Lefty, poor, poor Lefty.

Then dinner was served.

We sat around the table, my dad, my mom, me, Rosie, and we ate. In all honesty, I remember it as very nice.

Then the phone rang in the living room, and my dad almost knocked the table over to answer it, but I was closer, younger, faster, and programmed to answer it during meals. "Relax, Pa," I said, as he caught himself acting strange. "I'll get it, Pa. I always do."

I let it ring three times to let my pop fidget. Whatever he was acting strange about had to do with the phone. Maybe he was having an affair and tried to break it off, and she said she would call and blow the whistle. We didn't really know where he went during the day for his pretend job. When I picked up, the caller on the other side started breathing heavily, but it sounded like a man. "Stop calling here, Wally!" I shouted, and the guy hung up.

I was the only kid in high school who got prank calls from his principal. I caught him once after we'd been getting a string of prank calls. What I did is pick up the receiver right after the first full ring, but I didn't say anything. I just listened. So that when the second ring should have rolled around there was a noticeable silence, and a thicker silence after what should have been the third ring, and Wally couldn't take it 'cause he said, "Hello?" And I could recognize the mutherfucker's voice in a crowded auditorium.

"Who called, Son? You took an awfully long time," my Dad said in a fat-television-father-at-the-dinner-table-voice, without an accent.

"That wasn't a long time. It was a prank caller. Why you lookin' at me funny?"

He shook his head and shook on his normal face. "What do joo mean?"

"You look like that time you were trying to tell me where babies come from."

He laughed. "Thee boy ees funny. *Muy curioso.*"

As I crunched through the dark brown skin of the skirt steak, I taste the tiniest tang of lemon. "*Maravilloso, Mama. Esto me encanta, Rosie.*" My mom blushes as if I had said she was pretty. Rosie smiles.

"I sent a tape of you to 'Star Search'," says Dad.

"What!" I throw my meat onto my plate. "You're a..."

"Don't talk to your father like that," mother shouts.

"He shouldn't treat me like that...Ed McMahon's an idiot."

"Dat man's gone a long way for a sidekick. Hee'z struggled and won."

"Why do you do this shit to me?"

"Don't curse in this house," Dad shoots up from his chair for dramatic effect. "I doan want ju speaking like that at the table, with your mother and Rosa present. Why don't you listen to me for once. Jour life would be new and improved if you had let me take you to the Menudo auditions like I wanted to."

"I'd be a washed-up transsexual from a teen band." I grab Rosie by the arm. "Come on," I tell her. "Show's over."

She handles it perfectly and says nothing to me in the car. I wonder just how much my mom and Rosie have seen, what they do with all those secrets.

Dropping her off, I ask her if this weekend she wants to try and get into this nightclub called Faces. She's quiet, then says maybe we could go roller-skating instead. She tells me about other things juniors from her school do.

Not me. What I'd always wanted to have was a prime-time night on the town: dinner at a great restaurant, a carriage ride downtown, some club hopping, maybe a car chase—hell a carriage chase, maybe solving a murder then spending the night in a fine hotel, sexing in so many different positions that it takes us weeks to recover.

Of course, we both had curfews and neither of us had money. But even if we didn't and we did, these weren't things Rosie wanted to get bold for anyway.

I get a kiss when I drop her off.

I could never go straight home. When I was in high school, I spent a lot of nights circling and circling our block before pulling into the driveway, nervous like the first time I waited behind the curtains on the stage of "The Tonight Show," the spotlight waiting for me, the set ready.

I always entertained thoughts of leaving, just driving away, making it on my own, like I knew I could. But home was where the food was, where my mom was, the TV, my bed, cable. And my dad.

It is tough to explain who my father was because the different men he was are always filtered through the different men I have been. And thus he is always changing.

My father was an actor.

There was a time, when I was a very young man when I liked to say that, and then pause.

I would let the word "actor" unfold in your head as your experience has come to define it, let you picture a show or two, a face from a show, someone with Hispanic features. Do you see a handsome Latin Lover, a bandito, a gang banger, a man with a large mustache? Can you imagine my father as a leading man?

I never could.

Which still did not ease the disappointment of finding out that he was not a leading man.

My father was an actor in *carpas*, tent shows performed in Spanish and Spanglish.

He let the word "actor" build in my mind and in my stories about him, at the same time as the word "*pelado*" for me developed into a synonym for "punk."

And then one day when I was in 5th grade, he told me that when he acted he had been a *pelado*.

dreams

I don't know why he hadn't told me before then, or why he had told me that day in a practiced and nonchalant way as if we had just met and he was simply explaining what he did for a living.

There were times when my life would have been more merciful as a sitcom. Spending only a half hour picturing my dad as a punk on stage, grappling with what that word really meant, having in my mind as a definition only pictures of the kids who I had thought were punks, imagining what I must have looked or acted like when I was called it, looking for similarities, and placing them on my dad, in a suit, on some stage with a spotlight on him. Hoping that "I was a punk" could also be an idiomatic expression I had never heard that meant something like "I was a bad ass."

And I would compress, depress, and express all those wonderful moments that had led up to my life at that point, and there were certain scenes that I always went back to, I think triggered by each, maybe certain buildings I would pass in my drives around the block, past Bill and Betty's Bar, the abandoned Lithuanian Bakery, Tony's Supermarket, Unique Thrift Store, The Golden Dragon Chinese Take-Out, Jimmy's Barbershop, a turn of the corner, the alley and then homes.

And it takes years, and stories, and tidbits of information, and other peoples' recollections for a bit of history to resurface for me, for me to find out that the *carpas* were the Mexican version of vaudeville. And *el peladito* was a stock character. Plucky, living by his wits (which were sometimes questionable) and luck. He was part clown, part fool, part wise man, part court jester, all underdog. He was especially funny because of his use of Spanglish; and he was at times a caricature, at heightened moments, a symbol for the new breed of people who were growing up between the U.S. and Mexico, a new breed of half-breeds.

And maybe, just maybe my father was telling the truth, and he was one of the best *pelados* ever. And maybe it was just a matter of timing that Cantinflas and Tin Tan became famous. Maybe my father was born too late to do much with being a great, maybe even a wonderful *pelado*.

By the time his performances must have peaked, vaudeville and *carpas* had been almost wiped out by film. The earliest, most well-known performers had gone into film and even radio. And my father, perhaps, honed his craft alone. Thinking he could bring back the movement himself.

I can respect that, now.

But I also have to wonder how good he really was.

There are clips of him. From two newspapers, one from San Antonio, one from Phoenix. And he enjoyed explaining the details of the picture of him in costume. "Part of thee presentation ees thee tradition. The other part eeees my flare." Puddle-jumper, wide, flared pants—his innovation. A very short tie instead of the traditional long one. (And I'm sure this also afforded him a large store of phallic jokes.) A painted-on mustache and thin beard. Shoes with holes in them, long white stockings showing "because you have to stick to some of the old ways." And mittens hanging from his back pocket. "I was famous for my mittens."

He does not speak for the other picture. He simply shows it. He is dressed in a black, pin-striped suit, black thin tie; he is square jawed, hair slicked back, looking away from the camera and over our left shoulder, looking at something not too interesting, perhaps just resting his gaze there.

His name is under both photos, and if there were related stories, he didn't save them, or he didn't show them to me at least.

So I assume that he was either given a scathing review, a review so vicious, even *he* could not make it sound good by interpreting it for you, or he was a side shot, a side bar, just an incidental picture. Which might be even more tragic.

These, however, were not the end of the clippings.

When I was a baby, depending on the time of year, he'd dress me up like a pilgrim, a turkey, an elf, and create photo opportunities for the local newspapers, no matter how great or small, and sometimes local news shows or programs. There were many of these frozen moments. But then I got old enough to talk.

When he wouldn't listen to my protests, I started to swear on camera or shoot the finger at photographers like the older kids at school shot at me.

His next wave of clips were because of the house, but he also made the news for stopping a fleeing burglar, returning lost money, shaking Jimmy Carter's hand. There was a gold-framed photo of Dad when he was a contestant on "The Price Is Right" (He won a set of skis, which he sold. He didn't make the final showcase showdown.) and a framed personal rejection from "Jeopardy," signed by Alex Trebeck. Dad highlighted the key phrase: "We would lose too much money with you as a contestant." And all those pictures of Ed McMahon.

Then there is my father who won the lottery. Not *the* lottery. But *a* lottery.

I never even knew he bought tickets. And then one day, there was money.

Then there existed brochures on certificates of deposit, mutual funds, and stocks. I had to translate them. I was in 6th grade. He never let me see the official papers from the lottery, though. "I doan want jew 2 know zometing that could get jew keednapped," he told me with a straight face.

One day he looked like he'd cashed a hundred thousand dollar check. Not a million. I never saw that look on his face. And the way I thought of him then, I figured he *could* win a million dollars but never get or keep his hands on the prize. He said he would keep his job "because work made the man." This was before he got the brochures. He got together my college fund then quit his job. Then he bought the set of "Leave It to Beaver" and turned it into our house, using my college fund.

I figured he bought the house so he could get back in the public eye, which seemed slightly un-insane.

And sometimes Pop would forget he won the lottery and tell people that he'd won Publisher's Clearing House Sweepstakes and that Ed McMahon had delivered him a fat check. I didn't mind that lie. I got a kick out of picturing McMahon cruising through our neighborhood in a van with a million bucks, like a visitor from outerspace.

No one had a Neilsen Ratings Box where we lived. Cabs didn't cruise for fares. There weren't any Automated Teller Machines or health food stores, and *el carnicero* had dead, skinned animals hanging in his shop window. At the end of our block was a run-down abandoned bungalow whose graffiti evolved with the neighborhood: The Latin Disciples, The Latin Kings, Bishops, Saints—a regular Vatican IV.

Since I'd stopped helping him and our neighborhood had gotten too run-down and dangerous for even the bravest tourist to stop by and take a picture (the house was getting run-down too), Dad hadn't been in the news for a long time. This meant he was becoming a little too interested in my stab at comedian-dom. But I was gonna be as selfish as he was.

When I was a kid, he'd have heart-to-heart monologues with me and say, "Joo gonna haff to make it on jour own sum day. Joo know dat, Yoon-yer. There's no money for joo after I die. Thee money that fell on my lap is evaporating as we speak.

Eeetz flying out the fridge when joo leave the door open too long, spraying out thee lamp that's on when no one's in thee room. Joo gotta make money after joo get out of high school." And this he told the kid who busted his skull trying to correctly translate the complicated forms he showed him. I would stay awake at night, worried that my dad would get in trouble because I interpreted something wrong. He never let me even look at the lottery papers. All I knew was that there was money, and I knew where it was going to disappear before it would get to me.

"I know you smart," he'd say to me, "I know you know someteeng about thee money. But you doan know that eets all a trick on us. The lottery says they goin' to give you one million dollars. They make you think you a millionaire, like you can buy a manshion, beautiful cars, go on glamorous vacations, but they only going to give you fifty thousand dollars a year for twenty years. And then they going to take out tax, even though it's all run by the gobernment anyway, the gobierno still wants tax—that's seventy-five-hundred dollars. And you can't keep jour job because the other workers think you're a big shot then. They say you should give your job to someone who really needs it. They say they don't believe you won the lottery 'cause they never heard about it on the news. You tell them you just don't want your kids kidnapped. They say you're lying one way or another. You either always been rich or you're still poor. You can't keep working. So if you want a little more than forty-two thousand five-hundred a year, you gotta sell part of the pot. You get more upfront but less later, so the checks get smaller and smaller and then boom— you back to middle class."

But my dad didn't have middle-class obsessions or vices like smoking, drinking, a little whoring. No, I remember him blowing money on installing real plumbing into his dream house 'cause the toilets were props. Adding the cooling and heating systems that the actors hadn't needed.

My dad thought the den would be a perfect room for me because it was the room on the show with the books in it. "My son should be smart," he used to say to me and pat my head when I would still let him get that close.

My father gives me a heart-to-heart monologue when I get back home, in the Cleaver's den with the corroding bookshelves that Jerry Mathers leaned on between takes, the original prop books on the shelves: Victorian Poetry, Charles Brockden Brown, Nathaniel Hawthorne. Someone's written "Stinky" under Sonnet #152 in a Shakespeare book. I think it was The Beaver.

"Eeet ees our destiny to be famous. I wish it was not too dangerous to tell you who my father was, Junior," my father says. "He put stars in my eyes, cha-cha-cha in my head, zoom lense in my heart. He must have already been famous when he fell in love with your young, poor, grandmother—so beautiful, her long, black eyelashes, capuccino skin, her little hands scrubbing the floor, selling matchsticks. He married her and gave up his fame. He preferred happiness with a poor, young Mexican girl, until he was murdered by the forces that be. The forces that could not deel weeth their hero mixing his semen with such a lowly woman. And we have been happy so long that it is time for us to rise again, to reclaim our fame."

And what kind of son am I to have to wonder if he was telling the truth or acting? To suspect he was confessing that he was the bastard child of Ward Cleaver? Or just illegitmate? Was he telling me Gram had been raped? Or that he ripped her off for the money for the house? Maybe he robbed a bank, peddled drugs? What kind of kid was I to think this stuff? What kind of son was I to not believe the shit about the lottery unless I could see the paperwork? And even then...

I'm the kind of son who can't write two more jokes after that. I'm the kind of kid who promises and *will* write 22 the next day.

And if I had found out that night, two years before I investigated the issue and found out that the house was a fraud, that in fact, the two sets that had been used for "Leave It to Beaver" were accounted for, one on the Universal movie lot, the other having become the house for "Marcus Welby, M.D.," if I had found out that night that even my suffering was not as glamorous as I had hoped, I would not have been able to write those almost two dozen jokes. But I was spared that. I learn that truth when I am ready, when my suffering has been better put into perspective.

So instead, I slip to sleep in the den, flipping off in my bed. My thumb automatically pumping the arrow-up button, switching to pre-set channels. There in the dark, alone, the TV projecting on my wall, I slip between sleep and waking, not sure when one ends and the other begins, mixing in my head the frequencies of the dreams and the subconscious of the TV. Killing time between performances.

OPEN MIKE NIGHT II

Sixty jokes after I met Jester, I was back at Primo's, standing at the bottom of the three steps to the stage, waiting for the cue to climb up. I felt that little ant crawling around the middle of my chest where I think my trachea begins, the little ant crawling faster and faster, its sweat making my mouth taste coppery, me feeling a tingle when my teeth clacked.

The spotlight felt warm. And I could feel rays leaving my body to form a glow. "Thanks, Stinky," I tell the emcee. I leave the mike on the stand, and one move blends into another. "I know you don't recognize me from TV, but that's not my father's fault. He pulled some strings and got me an audition with Menudo. Does anybody remember Menudo? They were those four little punks in Spandex who sang teeny-bopper love songs in Spanish."

I spotted Jester's shiny noggin near the back of the room and next to him a head of big, blonde hair. His Blonde had on a long, shiny white coat that reflected the dim light.

"I was mad 'cause I wanted to be Speedy Gonzalez instead. But my dad kept saying, 'No, Stupid, he's a cartoon."

This was just an open mike. It should not have been a big

deal. But it was. It wasn't the "The Tonight Show," but it was tonight. It wasn't "Late Night," But it was late, for a school night. Visions of Cheech and Chong flipped through my head, Freddy Prince, "Feelink Goooooood," Charro, "OOOOcheeee Cooochie," Nurse Consuelo from "Marcus Welby." No, she wasn't funny. "Chihuahua! You folks need more booze." The audience cheered. "I'm buying everyone a drink. Waitress, one Bacardi and Coke, and three hundred straws please."

The tables were set comedy-club-regulation close, so people arched their backs over their tables, away from Jester as he rubbed past them, leading Blondie towards Rosie and our table. Jester had the power to analyze an audience in one glance and spot my girl in a crowded room. People ducked away from Jester's pelvis but he still got a few folks in the back of the head.

"I spent last summer updating the classics of literature." I imitate a rapper, "I turned MacBeth into..."

With her coat off, it looked like the Blonde was sitting there like a newspaper ad, wearing only a bra.

When it was over, the bottoms of my earlobes tingled. It was nice and loud as I climbed down from the stage. But I was smart enough to know it'd been mostly brute force this time.

A Bacardi and Coke was waiting for me at the table, and the Blonde was better than naked. She was wearing a white bikini-type of top with swirls of glitter. She had her shoes off with one leg under herself and the other on Jester's lap. Baldy was messaging her foot with one hand and working a drink with the other. When I shook his hand, it was warm from the friction. I wanted to say "You can get athlete's hand from that," but then I thought she might never let me do it. "T-O, this is Farah."

"Great set, Mr. Aztec Love God," she told me.

"Yours too," I would've said if I was still on stage, but I wasn't so I say simply, "Thanks."

Farah was Miss-America-playmate-of-the-year-runway-supermodel hot. Not that Rosie wasn't pretty. It's just that she was kind of boring. Of course if she'd worn Farah's top, with Farah's white leather micro-mini skirt, white hose, electric blue eyeliner, blue mascara, and fuchsia lipstick, Rosie would've fit any teen-age boy's definition of ultra-hot. But then we also would've been different people.

"Sorry I'm a little late, kid," Jester said. "I had a few technical difficulties."

I avoided looking at Rosie and said, "No problem." So much for playing this off as a coincidence. "What did you think of my tribute to Mexican comedy on TV?"

Six-foot-tall-and-bald shook his head. "Cheech and Chong were never on TV. And Chong's a chink. Maybe you and Hon Cho can get together and do an updated Cheech and Chong thing. Update that literature. Or maybe you and Hon Cho can get together and do Charro. Otherwise you got three short acts that don't fit together. I like it when your first joke has got something to do with your last joke."

I sit and say, "So I guess I blew the audition?" I say this without looking at the Bald and the Blonde—which is a great name for a bad sitcom. I sip from my drink, and it's got too much balls. I squeeze some of the lemon into it. I stare at the back of Rosie who's straining her neck to stay facing the stage as we all watch the car-accident on stage, some poor bastard who's saying this or that about his job at the bank, and everyone's watching, thinking the same thing. Vultures they can be, sadistic, thinking, "My life might suck, but I'm sure glad I'm not this poor bastard bombing on stage."

"Did you ever graduate?" Jester says.

"Huh? Why?" Over the drone from the banker, I thought I heard him wrong.

"'Cause I can't imagine you ever listening to one of your teachers. You're gonna do whatever you want, no matter what people tell you. You need to focus, focus, focus."

Farah leaned over, placed her hand on my knee and said, "You really looked good up there." Blood rushed to my head so fast it stirred up my stage-buzz.

The crowd gave up a crack of laughter. "One's a good year, the other's a great year," the banker said again and again until the laughing evaporated.

"You try to help a kid but he doesn't listen to what you say," Jester said. "What is it with you goddamn Puerto Ricans?"

"Hey, I'm not Puerto Rican. I'm Mexican."

"Whadda you got against Puerto Ricans?"

"I ain't got jack against Puerto Ricans. I'm just not a PR."

"You sure are one touchy Puerto Rican."

"How would you like it if I called you a...a...Czecho-slovakian?"

"I wouldn't give a shit. But if I was Puerto Rican, you can bet I'd be waving the Puerto Rican flag and talking Puerto

Rican every chance I got. So the question is 'Do you wanna be a star or just any other Puerto Rican?'"

"I'm not Puerto Rican, Son."

"Then for God's sake do a bit on 'em? 'Puerto Rican' is a funny word."

"So's 'Czechoslovakian.'"

"Say you're God damn half-Puerto Rican, half-Czechoslovakian. Build a persona out of it. You eat cottage cheese tacos. Nobody knows anything about the Czechoslavakian race. You can say whatever you want."

He just kind of looked at me. And I didn't want to say what I said next, but I felt I had to take a stand. "Puerto Ricans don't eat tacos." He laughed his ass off. And he's the only one laughing in the room, and he's laughing so loud even the guy on stage looks toward him. And Jester doesn't have to turn around, check, or look. He knows he's stolen the show. And he laughs even louder, I mean howls, and the comic on stage looks mortified, and then someone in the audience starts to laugh, and someone laughs at him laughing at Mortified who's doughy 'cause of Jester, and a whole group joins in only to be laughed at by another group of people at another table. And technically the guy on stage has everyone laughing. But of course he walks off. Which only makes everyone laugh even harder.

And THAT is the worst death I have ever seen on stage. The man was assassinated. Buried alive. Killed. By Jester.

The emcee comes out and says, "Ladies and Gentleman—Jester." And a spotlight shines on him. He turns and waves. People applaud. "We're gonna have a brief break while we talk Reno off the ledge. Please enjoy a drink, the restrooms are on either side of the room, please remember to tip your waitresses and waiters. Jester is the only rich person in the room."

And it's petty, and it's materialistic, and he's mean, but, man—Jester's The Shit.

The king speaks: "We're goin' across town to watch a gig—a *paying* date—I got Hon Cho. He's up around midnight. I'll spring for a few drinks."

"No," Rosie nags. "It's a school night. We have curfews."

"She's kidding, Jester. This is a bit we're working on." I gave her the eye. "I can make it."

"But Tio, darling," Rosie wraps her arm around my arm like a ball and chain. "I can't imagine what my parents would think if they saw me dropped off by a dirty, dangerous cab. I can only lie about so many things for you, Sweetheart." Jester and Farah looked at us like they were waiting for a punchline.

"I'm sorry, Jester," I staged a laugh, "but I just remembered that I'm leaving for St. Louis in the morning. I have to get some rest."

"You're pushing me, kid." He smiled and spread open his arms. "Tell me 'no' again, and I'll just have to cancel your pilot and look for you again in a few years." He leaned over and put his hand on the shoulder of the arm Rosie was holding, and he leaned that booze-scented head toward me. "Listen, what you need is a good role model. So this Friday I want you to catch my set. And I'm really gonna audition you. No more hints or suggestions. I think you know what I'm looking for. And I'm ready to take a chance on you. I can give you a five-minute floating slot. You can back out at the last minute, or you can try and make The Aztec Love God part of my stable." He dipped his hand into his multi-pocketed suitcoat and pulled out two gold tickets. With my free hand, I took both, but suspected I would need only one.

"Well, you're not inviting The Aztec Love God. That's kind of my ideal persona, that's the style I'm trying to work out here with all the different sets. I'll have to come up with a different, well, like you say, a definite focus. Somebody else."

"But the name 'The Aztec Love God" rocks. You can walk on stage in leather pants, a red shirt open down to your naval, a wig on your chest, hair slicked back..."

"Easy, Slick." And I was scared to tell him to fuck off because already I was greedy for those five minutes. "I'm coming out as Ghandi."

"Just be *somebody*. And bring some bail money because you *have to* stay out late afterwards.

Rose was full of thorns in the car.

"*I don't want anything to do with him.*" She mocked a deep full-of-shit voice. "If you lied to me about him, you've lied to me about other things."

"I've never lied to you about anything that would hurt you."

"So you HAVE lied to me."

"Just like you've lied to me."

"I've never lied to you."

"That's a lie right there. What you mean is, you've never lied to me to hurt me."

"Don't tell me what I mean. I mean I've never lied to you, and you just told me that you lie to me."

"Do you want to have sex every time I want to have sex?" She was quiet.

"Then on those times, by not telling me you didn't want to have sex but still doin' the deed—you lied to me."

"If you could tell, why did you have sex with me?"

"Because I wanted to have sex and you didn't say 'no'."

She slapped me on the shoulder. "You're an asshole."

"Every time you think that of me but don't tell me, you're lying to me."

"If I told you every time, I'd never shut up."

"You're lying now."

"Fuck you. Please shut up."

So I did. I'd made my point. I was even gloating inside because she realized I was telling the truth about all this lie business.

"So what have you lied to me about?" she asked. "What have you said to keep from hurting me?"

My smirk worked its way to my face and then blurted out, "MALO stole that test from Ravetti."

I heard her turn her head towards me. "What!"

Shit. By her tone I knew I had to lie now. "No. I'm fuckin' with your mind. What I've lied to you about is the times we do *it* and I don't want to do *it*."

"I can't believe you would let me get ready to practically organize a protest and then tell me that you're not only a liar but a thief, too."

"Shut up. I already said I was just fuckin' with you. I wanted to see if you'd believe the worst about me."

"Now you're lying to protect me I suppose, Mister Bacardi and Coke. Are you gonna have a Bacardi and Coke when you visit your Puerto Rican-Czechoslovakian cousins in Saint Louis? Was that lie to protect Jester?"

"I lied to his ass in saying The Aztec Love God isn't flying Friday night. The Aztec Love God is going on stage. I'm doing my act, my way. I'm stealing five minutes from Jester's mutherfuckin'-precious life, and if he doesn't like what he sees fuck 'em. We don't need him." I hoped saying *we* would bring her back to my side.

"You lie to everyone. You're just a big phony. You're just a piss-ass sell-out."

"Like you're not a phony. Are you the person who goes to Church every Sunday and sits and eats menudo with my family afterwards or are you the person who likes it when I eat her out?"

"Fuck you, you prick," she slapped my shoulder, "fuck you." She slapped my shoulder again.

"Or are you this person yelling 'fuck you' at me? Is your dad really a saint or is he the man who has two kids in Mexico from two different women?"

"I'm the person who hates you, you bastard," and she let out a scream. She started crying. "I'm like everyone else on earth who thinks you're an asshole." She tried to slap me in the face, but I blocked it with my right arm and swerved over to the wrong side of the street.

"I swear I'll plow right into the next car, you bitch. I'll drive right into another car."

She huddled into the corner of the seat and shuddered.

I straightened the car out on to the right side of the road. And I drove her to our trucking warehouse, without her asking.

She was still sobbing while she wiped off the makeup, the mascara that ran down her cheeks, the smeared red lipstick. "You are never seeing me naked again. And as far as our parents are concerned," she mustered, "I'm telling my folks you want to marry me. Tomorrow I'll tell my mom you proposed and I laughed and said we could get engaged after you graduate." I was speechless. The more paint she took off, the quieter I was, the more steady her voice became. She rubbed her face frantically with some swabs, stared into her little mirror. "And I'm going with you Friday. Maybe then they won't move you up to more drinks. Maybe then Farah won't ask YOU to rub her feet. Maybe dropping me off at twelve will make you think twice about going back to stay out late."

There's little a smart-ass-comeback can do to that. "You're crazy," was all I could say.

"And finally," she said, "I hate you, you stupid, dickless, asshole. I hope you die."

As pissed off and hurt as I was, I couldn't peel out after I dropped her off. I couldn't run over her sleeping parents' lawn. I slowly pulled away with my lights off, after she gently closed the door.

I was terrified that someday we WOULD get married.

All that passion. Touching each other without our bodies. In the mess of yells, all that truth. We had a hot love. Maybe too hot. Too all consuming.

I sped home with my cock hard and sticking into my pants like an arrow through my brain.

"'Caucasian-American Month' by Sam Kent"

With the approach of another Hispanic Heritage Month I have to admit that I'm jealous that our first observance of Caucasian-American Month was not a success.

Of course, I'm not blaming the organizers or supporters of Hispanic Heritage Month. I think *our* trouble started when the planning team got into its first argument over what we should call ourselves.

One faction supported the term "Anglo." Another supported "White." And yet another "Caucasian." In the end, we figured that having the word "Asian" in our name might help us gain some ground with already defined groups.

There were a few fringe groups whose suggestions hurt our credibility. They came up with names like The Man, Hyper-Aryans, Manifest Destiny-ers, Killer WASPs.

And then some "anonymous" people submitted suggestions like Pale Face Incorporated, Los Gringos, It's Okay to be Ofay, United Crackers. But we know who they were. And they just made us more determined to make Caucasian-American Month a success.

Though we didn't agree on *the* name for our group, we did at least settle on a name for the month. During other times, we'll use any one of the terms mentioned. In fact, if we see a really good friend on the street, it's perfectly acceptable for one of us to say to the other, "Hey, you, crazy Cracker, how are you?"

No, we didn't just catch static from minority groups (Come on, admit that you submitted at least one of those "anonymous" suggestions. Even if you didn't, you guys made up the terms.) and radical factions in our own group.

A lot of famous Caucasian-Americans simply did not want to help us.

This forced us to borrow a tactic from our Gay Caucasian-Americans (GCA) chapter. We are in the process of "outing" white people who did not embrace their heritage.

So let it be known that Bill Clinton is White! Even if he doesn't seem to want to admit it.

I personally wrote several letters asking President Clinton to author an introduction for our display titled: "George Washington—First White Male President."

He never called or wrote me back. So that idea was shot. My mistake was counting too much on politicians.

Since a lot of White Presidents have done so much good for the country, I decided and convinced the committee that our first heritage month should focus on political leaders. If you think about it, white men have contributed *a lot* to the development of our country. White men wrote the Declaration of Independence. White men wrote the Constitution. White Thought has really shaped our nation.

We really needed a focus, too. Without one, where would we start? White men discovered electricity, invented the automobile, the personal computer....

Our first plan of attack was to contact all the living White Presidents, all the White governors, all the White Senators, and representatives. But this amounted to over 500 people! 500 live and active White politicians. I was moved with pride. We were inspired to tackle the hard work it would take to contact all of them.

We even flirted with the idea of a Million White-Man March. But then no one got behind our program.

They all had excuses. All that work, and what help did we get? Nothing.

I'm just a family man trying to get by, trying to give my kids something to be proud of. And what happens? We get looked at funny. We get nasty letters. And we get called names.

I know what *they* think. I can tell when I visit them personally. I see it in their eyes. To them we're just a bunch of guys who missed the boat.

So Caucasian-American Month came and went without so much as a murmur.

Can you tell me which month was Caucasian-American Month?

No.

This was not a good year for us, but we are not going to go away. Someday, you will feel our presence.

I stay motivated by reminding myself that if you *really* look at it, even if it is unofficially, *every month* is Caucasian-American Month.

Happy Caucasian-American Month, America.

THE DEATH OF
ANTONIO MARQUEZ

In homeroom the next morning, Mr. Bavilsic skipped from "Manning" to "Nazarine" during roll without pausing to confirm my existence. It shouldn't have mattered to me. I still had 16 covalent bond problems to figure out for Chemistry, and if his mistake showed up as an absence on my report card, I could always prove I was here. But still, I raised my hand. Bavilsic ignored me. I kept my arm raised until the bell rang. Then I grabbed my books and walked out of the room. This was yet another fecal bit in a morning full of weird shit.

The other strange incidents were that there was a brown El Camino parked in my assigned spot; Kent simply ignored, didn't give me a demerit when I walked in late for first period; I hadn't seen any of my MALO friends; and no one had said "Hi" or "Wus up" to me. In and of themselves no one "incident" was a big deal. But all these incidents piled together seemed very strange. They even made the between-class-buzz in the hallway seem sinister, like everyone was plotting against me.

No chemical changes occurred during Chemistry. Everything stayed relatively the same during Physics. One way or another, I'd become invisible.

When the lunch bell rang, kids just walked around me in the hallway.

I waited as the juniors and seniors scurried towards lunch and intramurals, while the underclassmen dragged their feet to their next class. I paced at the intersection between the two hallways joining the two wings of the building where I would have to bump into one of my cohorts.

I turned and caught a glance of "A" as he hurried by. I called his name and ran after him. Either he didn't hear me in the crowd or he was trying to avoid me. I lost track of him around the corner. The hallway thinned out, students disappeared into classroom doors like bouncing molecules falling down holes. It was like "A" had jumped into a locker. Vanished.

I walked classroom to classroom.

Through the little square windows reinforced with thin steel crisscrossing strands (I guess the wire in the glass was so that if someone shattered a window, shards wouldn't fly), I saw underclassmen falling asleep in class, remembered how hungry I would get waiting for the seniors and juniors to finish eating so we could fight over their leftovers.

Usually, teachers patrolled the halls to make sure everyone was either in class or eating in the cafeteria or sitting in the gym or on their way to one or the other. No loitering in the halls. But that day no teacher bugged me in the hall. I wandered from door to door, looking through the little glass squares like I was strolling through some crazy museum with 3-D displays. History with kids' mouths open, frozen in time. Algebra with Xs in kids' eyes. French mind-sucks. I came to an empty classroom with the lights off and the chairs still at attention, facing the blackboard. I walked in. Just like I thought. There was "A" at a desk in the corner of the room, eating a sandwich. He looked at me like I was the principal and froze in the middle of a bite.

I stared at him.

He stared at me with bread in his mouth.

"What's up?" I said.

He shook his head and chewed.

I let the door close and walked out of the vision of the door window but stayed a few desks away from "A."

"'k' is gone," "A" said.

"What?"

He swallowed. "No one's seen him. He's gone."

"Maybe he's sick?"

"No. I'm sick. Something bad's going on. Something really bad."

"I know."

"You know?"

"Sure, Bro."

"What do you know?"

"That something bad's going down." I stood and moved a desk closer to him.

He stopped chewing. I moved back, to let the man eat.

"No one the fuck knows where 'k' went," "A" said. "Outside of...our group...no one says they know him. Never heard of him. The rest of the guys are scared to keep asking for him. Like they might disappear next."

"That's stupid."

He was quiet.

"He's just a freshman. They still have to sit alphabetical order in every class; he's gotta be one of the last kids in class. Maybe no one notices him."

He looked around, put his sandwich down, and looked in the desk, under the desks. Finally he addressed me in a whisper.

"'B' checked 'k's' homeroom teacher's roll. 'k's' not on there. He's not in anyone's gradebook or even the school directory."

"Don't get crazy. He's too new to be in the directory. Our mistake..." And he stared at me when I said, "our," "was not to have a stat sheet on every member."

His eyes puked. "I don't want my name on any kind of list." He gobbled his sandwich.

"Did he hang out with anyone from school?"

"With as many people as you hang out with from school."

"We should'a been more of a friend to him."

"Well, maybe he did something for us to be his friend."

"Like what?"

"Like maybe that dumb Puerto Rican kid wanted to be our friend so bad that he admitted...something. Maybe he thought he was getting us out of trouble." I was quiet. "He's not that stupid? S'that what you're thinking, 'D'? He's as bad ass as you are. As slick as 'D.' You wouldn't disappear for someone, but now you got two punks that have vanished for you, Bro."

"Fuck you." He filled his mouth with food. "People don't just disappear," I said.

"Well then, we know the first person who did. And I don't want to be the next. When I disappear from this dump, it'll be with a piece of parchment in my hand. I think we better cool it with this Monty Zuma shit." And this he said nice and loud. "That ol' boy's been conquered."

I wished I could have called him a pussy and mustered a third nut to rally the troops, but yeah, I was scared, too. I was willing to be a sheep to earn the sheepskin. When I'd rallied the troops before, I might have rallied them out of existence. Before opening my mouth and letting the right words come out, I stepped out of that class.

Brother Nummel was leading some underclassmen into a room. The last time I'd seen him he threatened to give me an "F" if I didn't turn in a late essay. That'd been several days before. I ran up to him and said, "Hello, Brother." He looked at me. He was holding the doorknob, about to close off his classroom. "I want an 'F.'"

"Do you have some place to be?" he asked.

"Give me an 'F.' I demand to see you open your gradebook to my name and write an 'F' next to it."

"I'm going to shut this door. If you are still out here when I look, I will kick your ass."

He slammed the door.

I was left to my own devices, but a joke or a wisecrack wasn't enough at that moment.

I wandered the checkered painted floors, the bright yellow walls of the hall, the light brown steel lockers. I wandered looking into windows, watching *Them* teach the kids, those sophomores, freshmen, until the bell rang, and we seniors were done eating. Students swarmed the halls, with their buzz, sending each other messages about how hungry they were, how bored, how far behind in their school work. And the seniors and juniors had to go to class, to take up the seats left open, to get the refreshed teachers, well fed, with some coffee in them.

Time for the next class.

My body knew which way to go, "After that bell, I move down the hall with the brown checkered floor, the one with the blue walls, to the steps, past the glass doors leading in from the street—do not bolt out the doors—to the orange wall where the freshman lockers meet the senior lockers. The smaller, scared creatures are freshmen," it led me, "to the first floor, and we get the books with the dark blue cover, with our name written on the soft white side."

Facing my open locker, not sure what I should carry with me to show I cared about my next class, Mr. Autruck walked in from the outside, leading a tall, dark man with tight curly hair, in a camouflage T-shirt, leading him down the orange hall. The man looked young, late twenties, early thirties at the latest, big chest, big arms, small waist, maybe a boxer, a weightlifter at the least. He looked too young to be a dad and too old to be a brother. The between-class-noise dwindled as Wally got closer, jingling his ring of keys, as more people noticed the powerful man quietly following him, carrying a black bag, daring us to bump into him. We moved closer to our lockers and out of their way. We stared into our lockers for answers, pretending to arrange and move so many important things, but we shuffled quietly enough to hear anything that might be said. No adult was led to a kid's locker unless the kid had died or been kicked out. It took a few pockets of guys ignorant to what was going on a little longer to shut up.

"This was your son's locker," Wally said. It was above another freshman who stepped away from his locker and slammed it, gripping his brown lunch bag. He scurried off to the gymnasium and the freshmen in other parts of the building. He had news to spread.

The man nodded.

Wally opened the locker with his master key, and the man started emptying "k's"—I couldn't call him that anymore—the student's Spanish, Algebra, History books into a large workout bag. We all bought our own books. And I wondered what this man did to pay for his son's tuition. What he'd thought he was getting his son into and what he thought now.

And it was as if we would all be late for class and lunch, hanging on for one word of explanation, to find out what his voice sounded like. But all the man did was shovel the books and papers into the bag, the notes his son had carefully copied, the handouts in some kind of order, all shoved in the bag. He worked quickly and finished by ripping off the pictures of women from magazines that the kid put up to decorate his locker, all ripped off.

The crowd evaporated and never looked directly at the man, Autruck, or the kid's books. I wanted to be late. I needed a demerit for being late, one more and I'd be on detention on

Saturday, but at least that was something. And I thought the teachers were right. All my potential and I was blowing it, misusing it, wasting it.

I was the last kid in the hall as the man and Wally talked near the doors out of the building. I saw him walk away and not turn his back as Wally said and repeated something to him.

All my potential and I was just a punk.

I slammed my locker. I ran towards the gym, where the freshmen had now moved for intramurals.

One of the brothers was holding open the gymnasium door to let stragglers in. He put his hand up to stop me. "You got..." was all I let him say, pushing his arm away, shoving past him. Some kids were on the court playing basketball, still wearing their damn ties. The bleachers were full of freshmen.

"I'm here today!" I shouted at their noise. "Look at me," I shouted and waved my arms, "I'm here. I am Antonio Marquez. Look at me. I'm here." And there weren't any cheers. Some of them looked at me, but in the din of feet shuffling, their mumbling, only a small immediate circle of kids playing ball in front of me could hear, would look at me long enough to maybe miss a shot.

"I am Antonio Marquez. I am here today." And no one cheered. There wasn't a stampede of soldiers running to stand up with me. "Marquez, Marquez," I yelled. And even the tug at my arm was much lighter than I hoped it would be. Much lighter than I'd imagined. A weak pull, really, is all it took.

DIDACTULA

Brother Love rides a motorcycle, sports a cross on his helmet, says Jesus was cool, doesn't make the sign of the cross after "accidentally" swearing. His acid trips must have been of a divine nature. "High School Counselor," God told him, "That's where it's at. You meet the next generation after the establishment's teachers have spurned them, man."

He hits me with a battery of tests.

1. Would you rather plant a tree or read a book?

Brother Love has decided that my problem is I need direction. He's filed some papers on me to keep the school from sending me to a mental institution if the tests I take prove I'm nuts. This paperwork goes into my fat file, and if life is fair, I say, someday they should let me include my headshots and a rebuttal.

2. Would you rather take a walk in a park or spend a day watching baseball on TV?

I cross out their question and scrawl in, in my sloppy handwriting which dips and flies along the small white space between questions: I would rather write a joke than eat.

I add more.

3. Would you rather be given head or eat pussy?

4. Would you rather have her on top or be on top?

5. Would you rather steal a test than study?

Then it's too late to erase the smart-ass shit I've smeared on the paper. There's nothing else to do but hand the sheet to Brother Love, 94 questions too soon.

And he just stares at me from his chair which he's moved from behind his desk to in front of his desk, next to my soft, black, vinyl Lazy Boy to make it seem as if we're equal, that he's not an authority, that I can talk to him, that he's willing the share the secret contents of all the psychology manuals on the shelves behind his desk, the contents of the college information guides on the shelves on this side of his desk.

"So what the Hell is your problem?" Brother Love says there with his ponytail, talking tough with me which was supposed to say to me that though he was "cool" he also meant business. "Let's just cut through the B. S. Wus up witch you, Bro?" And he knew the lingo. "Do you know what you're throwing away?"

"I'm not throwing anything away. I'm trying to make it all count for something."

"Getting kicked out of school is not the way."

"Am I kicked out?"

He let my question fill the room.

"Brother Nummel sent you here because he's full of love. He could've declared you E7—CRAZY. That's like putting you on detention for life. Brother 'N' must think you have potential. Brother 'N' cares."

"What happened to the Puerto Rican kid?"

He twisted his face and looked like he was gonna spit. "The Puerto Rican kid?"

"This is like some bad 'Twilight Zone' episode."

"No, Marquez, this is straight up real life, man."

"Don't call me that."

"Call you what?"

"My name is not 'Marquez.' It's 'Arterio Gonzaga'."

"Holy smokes! You got a lot of balls to try and make me think you've gone off the deep end."

"Don't use clichés on me. What happened to the Puerto Rican kid?"

"It's time for you to worry about your own ass, MARQUEZ."

And I don't say anything and he doesn't say anything. And I'm not gonna say anything first. So we're quiet. But he is not uncomfortable. He's studying me, probably reading my body language, which I think I can control, but he might be able to read into my control.

My ass sliding on the vinyl cushion sounds loud as hell. I try not to move.

My ass cheek gets numb.

We are still quiet.

I sit still until my entire ass is numb. Then it gets past the point of uncomfortable silence, for me, to a logical silence.

I must speak next.

"I stole the Biology test."

I didn't think I could tell him. But it felt like I was just asking for a glass of water or asking him how his day was. I expect everything to be all right because it was so easy to say.

Brother stares at the floor, all quiet. "You can't possibly realize what you're throwing away," he says again to me, but this time like he's reading it off the floor, raising his head to look me straight in the eye. And it dawns on me. All that work. All those people leading up to me. In a flash I see them all lined up, small brown people falling on barbed wire so I can cross safely over them, shovelling dirt to build my school. I see them all, like in Cortez's dream. And I want to cry. But I won't.

"You can probably get into any college you want." He swivelled in his chair. "You got the grades, you're Hispanic, you can get the recommendations...if you pick them carefully."

"Oh, shit. I wish I hadn't told you anything." I throw my hands over my face. And I mean it.

"But you did."

I eat my tears. "Then here it is," I say straight on. "I stole the Biology test. My fingerprints are all over Ravetti's desk. My answers are all over the school. I saved him all that red ink." This is my spell to summon 'k' from the grave.

He was quiet. Stuck his thumb knuckle in his mouth. Fidgeted.

"Brother, can you be the Antichrist if you don't wanna be? I mean, if Christ didn't want to be Christ, could he have decided not to be Christ? Did HE have free will? Can we choose not to be the Antichrist?"

"And delusions of grandeur! Satan was guilty of too much pride."

"Sometimes I think I got it all. Then sometimes I don't give a shit. Lots of times I get this sinking feeling that once I get my shit in shape, once I've gotten over trying so hard to be cool, once I've figured out I'm not as smart as I think I am, once I've given up trying to be the next Aztec Prince, Freddy Prince, Prince, figured out what I should do with my life every week day from nine to five...

"I'm kinda scared that right when I feel comfortable, I don't mean have all the answers, I mean comfortable with the questions, I'm scared that the day all that happens is the same day the aliens land."

"How many people have busted their ass for you to get to this chair and call yourself the center of the universe?"

"I didn't ask to be put here. And I don't like to be told I owe someone for something that I didn't ask for or I could've gotten on my own."

The counselor shook his head. We were both sliding in our chairs, our asses and chairs having their own argument. "You're a four-year free ride waiting to happen."

"The only reason THEY want to give me a scholarship is 'cause they fucked over some other Spic before me. Nothin's free in this country."

"In this world."

"In this galaxy, universe, in this infinity. If I take a scholarship, they can take it away from me."

"Bullshit. Whatever you learn is yours. They can't take knowledge away from you."

"But they can decide if I'm smart or not. And it's just if I repeat the shit they want me to know. I got the right numbers. They're just betting on whether or not I'll keep learning what they want me to learn."

"Maybe in high school, but college is a lot different. There are Mexican Studies programs, Multi-Cultural literature..."

"If it's a lot different, why are they letting me in? Because I can't hurt them with what I'll learn. Think about it. Before, it was 'cause my folks didn't speak English, so they were considered illiterate. Then it was 'cause they didn't finish high school. You needed a high school diploma to get ahead. Then it was 'cause they didn't go to college. And now they want to pay me to go? What's the catch? Where have they moved the invisible line to?"

He used "C's" real name and told me that "C" had done me a great disservice.

"Well, he was smart and got the fuck out of here early. And he's gonna blast through college quick and turn it upside down, and he's gonna get on the other side and then say, 'Now what?' Whadda you got for me now? And they'll have something. But he will kick their ass."

He opened his desk, pulled out a file and tossed it on his desk. "It's time to put up or shut up, Marquez. This is the test that will tell me where you're heart is really at because your mouth gets in the way of your thinking."

I opened my mouth. "Shut up," he said, and I did.

"This is your file. Obviously a smart guy like you thought carefully about which teachers you asked for recommendations."

I shook my head, "Yes."

"Well I have a letter of recommendation from one of these teachers, and it's one of the recs you signed a waiver on. Actually I'm not sure why this rec was kept on file because they don't have to be, especially since you waived your right to look at it. I'll get to the point." He picked up a photocopy of a recommendation. I couldn't see the name. I'd asked just about all of my teachers for one, and each rec looked like the other.

"The above student displays moments of promise when he channels his ruffian energy in a positive manner; however, he is very erratic. To put it in the academic vernacular: he has a 'bad attitude'." He looked from the paper to me. I don't know how I looked. I couldn't control my face, I'm sure. I felt heavy in my stomach, like I wanted to shit loose right there.

"It gets better."

And if I could've talked, I would've asked him to stop.

"In my estimation his potential is greatly compromised by his constant disruption of class. His smugness at the results of his outbursts leads me to conclude that he is not aware that his acts of insubordination are not conducive to a positive learning environment. When Marquez ruins the learning experience for other students, I firmly believe that he thinks he is actually helping the class. This must be true because he seems oblivious to the reactions of his classmates who have tired of him..."

He gave me a standing eight count. He could see me reeling from the blows, didn't bother to ask if I could keep fighting. I imagine him waving smelling salts under my nose, and maybe I asked him something or maybe he could read my mind by then because he said, "And no, it wasn't Ravetti. Someone whose test you can steal can't, even won't, fuck you over this bad. This was left on file so that someone would find it someday."

And they're bigger than I thought.

I don't know how long he let me stay there.

"The only person you can trust is me. You paid them back without knowing it, but now you've got to walk the straight and narrow. Understand? If you want to get out of here alive, you've got to play the game.

"They've got all the cards. Just make it easier for them. I don't think you realize just how hard you really make it for them. To hear you talk, you've got an idea, but it's gone off in the wrong directions. You've got to stay focused. You've got to turn the other cheek. You've got to love them, man."

And I probably stayed alone in his office long after the last bell. When I got into the parking lot, there were only a few teachers' cars left parked. All the kids had left. There was a folded sheet of yellow paper slipped under my windshield, with a heart with horns on it, a note from Rosie.

And I felt so tired, like I'd caught the bad end of a fight. My head was heavy, my legs wobbly. But even then, as I lay in my car, dying, it struck me that my badassness must be like water, and it must know when it's boiling and cooling off or frozen and melting because all I could think of was my old tricks. I was fucked up, ass kicked and all I could think was one thing: maybe Brother Love himself was trying to fuck me over. Maybe he was an evil genius who knew the only way to bust my balls at that moment. Maybe HE was the guy setting me up?

There was no way to go but the card in my wallet. Call Jester and make a new plan. I'd see his set in 40 jokes. It was 40 jokes to my new life. I'd have a few extra days to get my act together 'cause I wasn't about to go back to school, for a while at least. I needed to pad another escape route just in case...in case, my God, in case I didn't graduate. In case I didn't go to college. And I was counting just the jokes I could write down. Otherwise I was living a laugh a minute.

And no. I didn't hate my life. I just didn't envy it.

COMEDY DOGGIE BAG I

The Aztec Love God's Comedy Notebook
Joke Doodles
Joke sCRAP book
Non-Mex Jokes (-1)

3/12/86/#3 I asked my dad why he didn't worship Ricky Ricardo, who was Latin, instead of Ward Cleaver who was white.
Because Ricky Ricardo is not Mexican. He's Cuban.
But Ward Cleaver's not Mexican.
No, but he's not Cuban.
And that was that.

#10 I am Mad Don—the male Madonna.

#12 I had six personalities in my previous life. Then I died. I'm okay now. I'm not a schizophrenic anymore. But I sure hope those other guys live a long, long time and don't catch up with me. Especially the one who liked to eat ants.

#15 I was preconceived.

#16 I shoplifted a copy of a self-help book, but I never got around to reading it.

3/13/86/#2 I'm glad I made it through childhood with only a vinyl fetish.

#10 The Dumb Guy tradition goes way back. Remember Jethro from "The Beverly Hillbillies"? How about Jed from "Green Acres"? Barney Fife? Well, our show is just like that except we'll have two Dumb Guys, maybe even three. And there's enough money in the budget for a stunt.

#12 Russia wants Financial Aid. I'm all for giving them a student loan or some kind of work study deal.

#13 My friend's a chemist. He analyzed Slimfast and discovered it's made out of crushed PEZ Candy. Maybe they'll make a Tommy LaSorda dispenser that spits the shit out of its neck.

#15 I have a financial advisor. He told me I should've invested in IBM thirty years ago. I told him I wasn't even born back then. He told me it wasn't his fuckin' fault my parents didn't meet sooner.

#16 I have a financial advisor. The problem is, he looks like Mr. Haney from "Green Acres." By applause, how many people have ever watched "Green Acres"? I'm sorry, sir, I didn't ask who lived there.

COMEDY DOGGIE BAG II

The Aztec Love God's Comedy Notebook
Non-Mex Jokes

INTO THE AUDIENCE (The audience is always wrong.)

3/14/86 I am going to ask you a question, don't think too long, answer it quickly. You sir/ma'am...

#6 ...We are magically transported to the front of the Sears Tower which is now a giant chalkboard with a trigonometry question written on it. Who would solve the question first, me or you? (No, you're wrong. _____ would.)

　　　You sir/ma'am...

#7 ...If we were transported to another planet, who would miss gravity more?

#8 ...Who is a better conductor of electricity?

#9 ...Who could hold their breath longer under water?

#10 ...sustain a stronger electric shock?

#11 ...eat more glass?

#12 Am I better than Elvis?
I mean, if I really tried?

#15 I wish Christianity was still illegal. I'd be in the mob then. I would administer drive-by blessings. If I got in an argument with someone, I'd threaten to consecrate him. I'd shout, "I'll consecrate you—Mutherfucker" (swearing would be part of the whole illegal thing).

3/14/86/#3 Too much money makes you crazy. Look at the Tooth Fairy. Here she's got all this money, the power to fly, the power to sneak in and out of houses without being noticed, and all she's got to show for it is a ton of rotten teeth.

#5 Eavesdropping is what Adam had to clean up.

#8 Things are sure different nowadays. I remember when I was a fetus...

Hecklers
#14 I'm not used to an audience with class.
#15 I really wish this place would screen its customers.
#16 I'm shocked you're bald. I thought all assholes had hair.
#17 I had a shirt just like that—then I regained my sight.
#18 Were you recently deinstitutionalized?
#19 This man is drunk and ready to take advantage of himself.
#20 Your mother.

A MODEST PROPOSAL

"Junior, get down here." There was an English-speaking man in the house shouting orders at people. My father had been speaking with an accent so much lately that I wasn't sure whether or not to listen to the orders (they were very clear and very loud) or call the police. "¡Ándale!" Ah yes, Spanish. I realized that the man yelling was my father, shouting like he must have shouted when I was conceived. "I'm a loved baby," I thought to myself. "I'll bet both of my parents came when I was conceived."

"Are you deaf?"

"Yes." I pause long enough for him to suspect I mean "Yes, I am deaf," then add, "I'm on my way." There was no point in arguing with me about this. It's something I can gloss over and keep saying, "but I had to pause, doyouwantmetotalk withoutpausingbetweenwords? WithoutbreathingIcoulddie. I talk so much I could drown talking." But then I'm wasting time preparing an argument I won't have to use 'cause Dad's good at this by now. He'll just overlook that Yes-I'm-deaf bit and add it to my account, to whatever it is he's shouting and speaking clear English about, and I must be really feeling cocky 'cause I'm wasting time I should be using to assess the situation. I'm wasting time thinking of this shit (poo just mentioned) instead of figuring out what I might have to be getting out of and imagining ass-saving-scenarios.

He is at the bottom of the stairs. The phone is still vibrating from him having slammed the receiver, and he's staring at me so hard he stops me in mid-skip down the stairs, and the only reason I don't freeze in mid-air is 'cause that would distract us, and he does not want to be distracted, so he doesn't levitate me with anger. And when my feet hit the stairs, all of a sudden I want to do homework. He reads my mind and says, "Get down here." And he points at the couch and makes me fly there.

He paces back and forth, like he's trying to work off some energy so he can speak at just a yell to me and keep from hitting me with a stick or something. He's got a red robe on, light green-TV-dad pajamas, and brown Hush-Puppies slippers. He's got on all the gear that should make him look like some nice TV dad, but he is not afraid to kick the shit out of me. And he's only done that twice in my life, and by this time I could probably kick his ass back, but if I took a swing at him, my hand would freeze or turn to stone or the blood would drain from it and I would be impotent for the rest of my life. At least that's what it says in the Bible. And my dad's got this black sash around his waist, and it's dangling like he's some kind of third-degree-hands-registered-with-the-police black belt. He really looks invincible. And this is too serious to be about school. Maybe I blacked out and stole stuff. He was so mad this could be about only one other thing...

"That was thee Hernandez family." The accent means he's more under control, at least in control enough to control his accent. "Meester Hernandez to be exact."

And he lets this sink in.

"He said you and Rosie are goink to get married after jew graduate."

He let this sink in.

"How come I gotta fine this out from someone else?"

Sink.

"How come you gotta marry thee first girl who comes along?"

Sink.

"Are you two having sex?"

Sunk.

"I expect some kine of answer from you."

"I don't know what to say."

"Is she pregnant?"

"No. I don't think she's pregnant."

"She's not pregnant?"

"Did Mister Hernandez say she was pregnant?"

"No."

"She's not pregnant."

"You think you're in love with her?"

"I guess."

"You guess? Jew gonna get married for the res' of your life in a few months and you guess you're in love?"

"I don't know."

"Have you thought about this at all, hmmm? Listen, I'm a man. I want to talk to you frien' to frien'. I was young once, too. Do you think I was born old?"

I had to laugh 'cause I'd forgotten he wasn't born old. He was just old when I was born.

"Don't jew wanna be a comedian?"

"A lot of Jews are comedians."

"What's dat gotta do weeth jew?"

"With me or Jews?"

"With joo."

"I don't wanna be a comedian. I am a comedian."

"Den you gotta decide. Do jew wanna stay a comic or do jew wanna become a husband?"

I hadn't looked at the question that way before. I hadn't even thought of the question before. But, yeah, it made sense. Maybe my dad had wanted, maybe he could've been the best *pelado* ever, maybe if he couldn't bring back the entire form, he could keep one role alive. He could work every day on pretending to trip, on outfoxing city slickers, practice rolling his eyes. Maybe that was his dream, his logical, his rational dream before he donated his spurt of DNA to my makeup.

"So were you and ma goin' at it and then she asks you, 'R joo chure joo wanna feneesh thees?'" I wanted to say. Instead I said, "But being a father seems like such a beautiful thing."

He looked at me like I was the TV talking back. I accepted his stare without budging because I, after all, had not said anything bad or wrong, so I was merely waiting for him to answer my sincere question. I had no reason to squirm.

He stayed quiet. I tried to think as loudly as I could, "Was I a choice between being a *pelado* or becoming a father? Did I save you from a comeback with some trained monkey act? Which kid didn't we have in order to move in to the Cleaver's set?"

"Yes, it is."

I forgot what question I'd spit in to the world where my father swims. All that time, we'd been staring at each other like TVs facing off. All that time he'd been thinking of or going over an answer, which is how his DNA works in me too. Then he says, "Yes, it is!" The new motto for the year of The Father of The Year campaign—"Yes, it is!"

"No, I'm not," I interject a pause into my interjection, "going to marry Rosie." And with that I kill off a kid. And I'm gonna keep comicking—more kids dead—and I'm gonna pull out or keep my monkey covered every time I dive into a gene pool.

"Das good, m'ijo. Now you using your head."

Now I won't be using my other head to create heads.

"I'll splain everyteen to joor ma. Oh yeah, joo gotta call the school. They keep calling."

Killing kids is okay and missing school is okay.

That night I call the man whose voice the office will recognize as my father's voice. And I know exactly who my father is. Part of him is the man in front of me who put up the basic material. Another part of him is my signature which the school, the state, the government recognizes as the scrawl of the man who made me. Another part of him is the voice of the man I write a script for and ask to call places and say things my father must say. And I am the conductor directing all these moving parts.

My dad had no say in the matter. He didn't decide to abandon his dream of becoming a star. I decided I wanted to live.

And Rosie is nuts. This Rosie, I never knew she was into the grand spectacle. This makes it harder to divorce her. But I must. All the babies in me demand it. All the babies inside me want me to go on, insist on not living so that I can achieve our fulfillment.

SHARKDANCE

Jester's name was on the marquee at Side Splitters. When I showed our tickets at the door, a waitress walked Rosie and me to the table where Farah was sitting like a cat, her red shoes dumped on the floor and her red panty-hose-smothered legs curled underneath her. "Hiya, T-O." Farah stuck out her hand and I shook it. I could have sunk into the soft bed of her palm and never heard from reason again.

"Order anything you want. Jester cleared it. But there's one condition." She stuck the corner of the drink menu in her mouth while she studied me.

"What's the catch?" I asked.

"It's time you became a multi-drink man. Try this. It's a Long Island Ice Tea." She offered me a taste from the lipstick covered side of her glass. When I acted as if I would drink the whole thing, she play-slapped me.

"Stop it," Rosie reminded us of her existence.

Farah looked at Rosie as if she had just crawled out from under the table. "Why don't you order a mixed drink, Rosa?" Farah said.

Rosie picked up the drink menu and studied it. "I'd try a Vodka and Orange Juice," she said, "but I hear it's used for bleaching hair blonde. I think I'll order some wine." She knew the marriage bit could not work in the club with Jester or Farah.

Farah gave her a fake laugh. I changed the subject. "Do you know when I'm going up?"

She put her hand on my lap to answer me. "Well, 'T'..." That close, I could not only hear her words, watch her red lips, and smell her real Obsession, but I could also feel the vibrations of her voice through her hands, into my knee, and throughout my body. "...a few of his guys are up first, then Jester'll be up around ten. Then you."

"What? That would make me the headliner."

"He wants you to have a good audience. Besides, it's actually a five-minute set after the *headliner*. You are gonna look so good up there." She looked me right in the eye, and all I had to do was look her right back, focus my eyes with her eyes. I didn't have to be humble or funny anymore.

I remembered that Rosie was next to me. I turned, but she was staring towards the empty stage, straining to keep her neck turned.

The first comic, Aladdino, sucked. The Middle-Eastern strip of Jester's rainbow said shit about three humped camels, camels with hump implants, paused between jokes like he was waiting for laughs—and wait he did. The next guy was a 300-pound Antarctican who never said anything about his weight, and sure enough, all I could think was, "Man, this guy is fat." And of course, Hon Cho was pro.

But Tall-and-Bald rocked Side Splitters. All timing and persona. I see what he meant. "It's not what you do so much as how you do it. It's that it's you doin' it. Your persona."

Jester drew a line on the center of his head and said, "I'm sick of being called a dick behind my back, now I'm gonna live like one." He pointed his head at the audience, stared at them through the slit drawn on his head. After he panned the room once, he dribbled water out of his mouth. "The circumcision went wrong. I piss from the wrong spot." He looked up, squirted again. "My folks were too cheap to get a good doctor. They sent me to the same vet who fixed our dog. I came back like this, and Sparky came back without a tail. God, my dad was a dick.

"But being a dick has its privileges."

"Being a dick has its privileges." People were saying the

phrase in the bathroom, on the way to their cars, to the people at work. "Being a dick has its privileges..."

Farah said she'd heard most of the act a hundred times, but she still laughed like crazy. I was on the verge of tears. I didn't think people actually did that, laugh so hard that tears streamed from their eyes. The audience hooted and gave him a standing ovation. He stayed on after the applause died down. And then the dick introduced me.

"Dudes and Dames, I want to welcome a new Satan in the hell of comedy. He's a good friend of mine, a very funny son-of-a-bitch. He is Juan Valdez, Jr."

And 'cause *he* introduced me, the customary smattering of applause was louder than usual.

I smiled, kept my head lowered, tried not to spit out adrenaline, tried to remember a joke, peeked from side to side as I stepped to the mike.

"You don't recognize me, but my dad was the first Hispanic on American TV. You know—Juan Valdez, the dude who picked the coffee beans. Not many people know he was Ward Cleaver's love child. My life's been a Mexican version of "Leave It to Beaver." "Leave It to Burro," it should be called, starring me, José Valdez, as The Burro.

"Because my father was the bastard son of Mr. Cleaver, the producers of "Leave It to Beaver" let us live on the set.

"Being a Spic has its privileges.

"My job everyday was to clean the beaver droppings out of the living room. The Cleavers were the filthiest people you ever met.

"My mother got jobs cleaning other celebrity families' houses. She cleaned the Flintstone's house, the Rubble's house. The Addams Family actually paid her to dirty their house.

"That bitch Alice stole the Brady account from us. Stole the food right out of our mouths, that dirty Czechoslovakian. Yeah, she was illegal. But she was an ocean-back. She had to cross the Atlantic to get here. That girl could *swiiiiiiim*.

"On Sundays all the Hispanic celebrities would come over to our set for menudo. Cheech Marin would try to smoke the cilantro. Charro would always take the first bite and yell, 'OOOOcheeeee cooochie,' stand and wave her hips around like she used to.

"My dad still pulled some strings and got me an audition with Menudo. Does anybody remember Menudo? They were those four little punks in Spandex who sang teeny bopper love songs in Spanish.

"I was mad 'cause I wanted to be Speedy Gonzalez instead. But my dad kept saying, 'No, estupido. Hee'z a cartoon.'

"But it didn't matter. I had too much *cajones* for Menudo, even at eleven. 'The boy,' the audition dude told my dad, 'The boy has too many bumps in the outfit.' Boy, my father was 'peesed' off. He said, 'Yoon-your,' to this day he calls me Junior, 'Yoon-your, yew peesed me oooff. Eeef yew won't work, yew must get married.'

"So he promised me off to this girl from our Church. Bought me a red-velvet tuxedo and everything. Said I'd have to grow into it.

"My future wife's mom was a devout Catholic. In Spanish, 'devout' means crazy. For a honeymoon gift, mommy-in-law gave my wife an extra hour on her curfew. And let her wear makeup!

"The marriage almost didn't go through though. When I was walking down the aisle in my red-velvet tuxedo, her father stood up in the middle of the church and shouted, '¿Que? That boy, he has too many bumps in the outfit.'"

"Menudo!" Jester howled when I got off stage. "Menudo!" he said again and slapped my back. The crowd was still applauding when he got on stage to close out. "Ladies and gentlemen...Hoe-zay Valdez." I got a roar. Hands reached out for me as I parted the dark on the way to my table. I slapped some hands five, shook some hands, someone pinched my ass. "Menudo!" Jester shouted on the mike and got a laugh. Walking through the buzzing and humming crowd, them moving their legs for me while I was still two feet away, giving me thumbs up, walking through that multitude, I could feel the bones that come out of my back arch up and support my huge wings.

Farah kissed me on the mouth, sat me down. Rosie's glass of wine was still where the waitress had set it down. Farah rubbed her lipstick off my mouth.

"What happened to Rose?"

"I don't think she was feeling good. Never mind her; you were so hot. They love you."

The seating lighting came on, and the crowd started to dissipate. Strangers on their way out gave me a pat on the back.

"L.A. has got a hard-on for you, kid. You are a million bucks waiting to happen," Jester said when he was back at the table.

"If I go to L.A., I have to be back by twelve."

"Let's popsicle-stand this blow, Kid." Jester leaned over and dunked his tongue in Farah's mouth. It looked like she was making out with a mannequin.

She said good night to me, and us guys walked away.

"Isn't Farah coming with?" I asked.

"She's done with me for now. Tired from dancing all day over at Planet Men. She's always exhausted by the end of my act, so she goes to her place to get some rest, and I show up later and screw her brains out, or in. What happened to Rose?"

"She had a stomachache. I'm gonna check for her outside."

The doorman told me that she had asked him to call her a cab. "Was she upset? Could you tell if she was crying?"

"She wanted a cab, guy."

"My brother's name is Guy, I'm José."

"Don't worry about it," Hairless told me. "Just leave a message for her on her answering machine, something nice." I shrugged. "Relax, I know a rock'n bar with a high women-to-men ratio and an even higher looks-to-woman ratio." He shouted and waved at a cab on the other side of the street. The yellow car screeched to a halt and pulled a U-turn. "Now that's a cab driver."

"To Shark Dance, Vladamir," Jester told the driver, "to Shark Dance."

The cab stunk: bad cologne mixed with good cologne, cigarettes, our stage-sweat and patches of hardened B.O. or huge dandruff that'd fallen off people. My hands smelled like the mike, tinny, like beer tastes when it tastes like the can.

Jester made the driver laugh so hard he let us out of our fare and wanted to know when Jester's next show was.

I would have liked to have rested. Just slept. But there was no time for that.

Jester got out of the cab like he was a big muscle, a walking 72-inch bicep. Three or four people in line shouted his name. But we didn't have to wait with them under the thick rope rigging on the front of the place. The bouncer hi-fived Him and let us right through. Throng of people, lights, smoke, it felt like we were under a sea of House music with schools of babes and squids moving up and downstream, sharks and bait clustered around the dance floor. What I could see of the walls were covered with nets, starfishes, plastic sharks, neon lights. Jester scoped out the place like he was the biggest hammerhead. "Welcome to Fantasy Island," he said. He leaned toward me to make sure I could hear him over the music. "Tonight you are Ramon Cervantes, a headliner from Houston, one move short of breaking the big time. Just dive in, Son. Go with the flow. You're not bound by gravity anymore." He picked two drinks off a waitress's tray. She stopped and was about to yell, when he gave her a fat tip. He got the dark drink, and I got the clear one. The traffic pulled us upstream.

A cheer rose from a pocket of people near the far bar, a cheer for Jester. "Ladies and gentlemen," the deejay said over the music, "Jester has entered the building." Aladdino rushed to shake his hand, but Hon Cho pushed him out of the way. "I got too many ladies on my hands. Help." We passed the fat Antarctican. Clinging to the barnacle-covered bar was a short black guy who I guessed was Ram Bo, a bald woman, three six-foot-tall skinny, pale white guys. I floated at His elbow like lamprey waiting for shreds of meat.

A gorgeous redhead in a catsuit walked up to me and started dancing. She said her name was Calavera. I asked Jester to order me a premium-no-lead on the rocks and shoved my way to the dance floor, pretending I was a robot. Calavera giggled. She pulled me onto the dance floor and started spinning around as the ultimate mix of all time, "Native Love," thump, thump, thumped out of the speakers. "Dance rock feel the heat/rock to the rhythm of the native beat/come on." I jumped up and down and flailed my arms, clearing a small space for us. A hammerhead shark was painted on the floor, and we were dancing in its jaws. She laughed. I grabbed her arms and pulled her close to me. "My clothes are by Armani and my body's Jack LaLane/Tiffany and Portiere are telling me the time/this native love is restless and I'm just not satisfied." When she wasn't looking, I gave an exaggerated wink to a blonde in black, dancing with some guy in a suit. She smiled back. We continued eyeing each other behind our partners' backs under the boom, boom, boom of the blaring hundred beats per minutes.

After a couple of songs, all four of us left the floor, but the blonde was careful to stay near us. The redhead pinched my butt, whispered that she was going to order a drink. Blondie pointed toward the other side of the club. We met in front of the ladies room. She told me her name was Manalini Of The Cleaning Clock, Mana for short. She asked how I knew Jester.

"We've done shows together in L.A."

"I didn't know he had connections in Hollywood."

"No. L-A as in Louisiana."

She laughed and asked me to dance. A slow song was playing, so I pulled her next to me. She placed her hand just over my rear, where the curve begins. I pulled her close to me so that her breasts were crushed against my chest and put my hand on the middle of her butt. She asked if we could go to my apartment. All of a sudden I remember I'm just getting used to not having a curfew, or ignoring it at least. "We can sneak into an empty stall in the mens room." The moment I finish saying "room" I'm terrified she might take me up on this.

"We'll go to my cave," she says. "There's something about yours you don't want me to know."

And I keep thinking that no one should realize two fantasies in one night.

She's driving my car 'cause she knows the way.

She's talking. At least I see her red lips moving, laughing. And I must be answering 'cause she pauses, looks at me, responds.

I'm pressed against her and 'cause she's taller than Rosie there are tits where tits should not be, more tits than my fingers are used to knowing, less waist before more hips.

I feel the boiling adrenaline backing up to the bottom of my throat.

Finally, I'd be having sex in a bed instead of a car. No worrying about getting home. She'd even keep her makeup on afterwards. And I wonder what this woman is really like.

"Baby," Mana says to me, "I'm gonna show you something special." She kisses me at a red light.

We walk inside her place. I was expecting a cave setting. She had movie posters all over the room, pictures of comedians on one wall, a pinball machine in the corner. No waterfall, no apes.

Mana pulls me in and closes the door while she yells this: "I couldn't find what you wanted, Honey, so I brought this guy T-O instead, and from the looks of it, he's got a nice package."

"What?" I didn't know what the fuck she was yelling.

"Bring the shotgun and shoot it off while it's still hard." She turned the key in the lock, pulled it out, and dropped it down her top.

I tried to laugh, but it sounded fake. It really sounded like "heh, heh, heh."

And then Farah stepped into the room.

The moment I should have been the hardest, I went limp. She was barefoot, in gray sweat pants, and a white T-shirt. "Farah, what's goin' on?"

"I'm just here waiting for Jester to come screw my brains in." She pulled me next to her and kissed me, lapping at my lips with her tongue, gently biting my tongue, controlling when we went lip to lip or lap to lap.

"I wanted you so bad from the first day I met you. Don't you want me, T-O?"

I nodded. She led me by the hand to the futon, tells me to sit on the floor in front of her, below her, at her feet. I'm kneeling in front of her, and she stoops down to give me mouth, to rub her hands on my chest. She presses my shoulders, sits me down. Slowly siphons off her kiss, raises her head and pointed chest, raises her leg and puts the bottom of her foot on my face, right over my mouth, and says "lick." They smell like Opium, are soft. It's like rubbing her arm or ass on my face. There's no taste. She says, "That's what it's like to have a big dick on your face."

I spit.

"Relax." She rubs her foot against my hard on, presses it down, kneads it. Puts her other foot on my face. Pulls the bottom of her T-shirt out, rolls it up to her tits. They're shiny, round, with dark brown, wide tips. She rubs them together, leans toward me, grabs my face, brings both feet to my crotch. She opens her mouth over my mouth and rubs the inside of her big lips over my lips, soft, warm. She kisses me softly, flicks me, reaches down to my hard-on. "Nice," she says, "I'll let you know if it's big or small. Right now, I've decided that it's big." And it listens to her.

She stays bent, with her tits on her lap, rubbing my hard-on through my pants. My eyes are slit, and I can barely breathe through them. She reaches down my pants and moves my boner so it points up. She rubs the underneath of it. I'm sweating cum.

When I climax she presses her hand on the throbbing, and I can feel the hot fluid spit under my shirt. "This way it'll last a lot longer next time," she says. And it does.

FAKE ID's:
A MANUAL
FOR YOUNG MEN

It makes me feel good to fake the right documents, to rig the right pass to get me in the joints that for some reason only twenty-one-year-olds are supposed to pass in and out of as they please—as long as they got the cover price, are dressed right, aren't too drunk, and, depending on the joint, if they got the right look (but at those places I know that most twenty-oners, shit, most adults don't get in there. So many don't get in that most don't try. So I know better than to work that hard just to find out that I don't belong in there, that I wasn't studly or rich enough, couldn't order the right drinks for the right price for the lady at the end of the bar.)

And the ladies got it made. If they're pretty, they can get into any club as soon as they learn how to flirt. 'Cause most bouncers are just big palookas who giggle when a pretty girl smiles at them, says "hi," remembers their name. And the owners want pretty ladies in their club. And the fact that they might be in there is why guys like me try so hard to get in before it's time.

And if I strike out, that's fine 'cause this is all pre-game. I'm not even supposed to be Fuckin' in there. So whatever good thing happens to me is all extra-credit, a bonus, free, free, free.

There're all kinds of ways to get in. First off, young man, you gotta have the balls to try it. You gotta have the balls to accept rejection. Some bouncer might laugh at you. Some might get cocky with you. Some might try to confiscate your fake ID. You gotta remember that you are twenty-one. No matter what happens, you are twenty-one, you feel twenty-one. You look at a lady, and maybe she's smiling at you or maybe she's smiling at the guy behind you, either way, you gotta look back with that grin on your face and think "Yeah, I'm twenty-one." So you gotta keep in mind that this bouncer is doing YOU wrong. He's denying you your right. So act like it. Act a little indignant. You have to say, "I can't believe this. I always come here. Is Tony working?" There is always someone named Tony working at a club. And the bouncer will never go look for him. Don't get pissed off at the guy or pick a fight with him 'cause really the guy is only doing his job. Plus, bouncers bounce from club to club. You never know when you might bump into him again. And if you two brawl, he's bound to have more friends in the joint than you do. Remember, you can't get into the dump, so you probably don't know anyone anyway. Besides, he can probably kick your ass. Not my ass. But I won't fight him, for the reasons just cited.

You gotta remember too that this bouncer is still a regular guy. A man just like you, who was under twenty-one at some point, who gets googly over women, who likes a good time, who hates his job. You can say, "Oh well, what the fuck. I can't get in, I can't get in. God doesn't want me to go in there for some reason. Maybe my wife's in there waltzing with a Chippendale's dancer. You know a club where I can get in with what I got?" Ogle some women with him. Hang around the door for a little bit, shoot the shit. He'll either give you a helpful tip, feel bad and let you in, or the next time you see him at a door, you might have an "in."

The way to avoid this situation is to have the right papers in the first place. There are lots of legal ways to get fake IDs. And these'll work at about forty percent of the places you try, maybe fifty percent, as long as you got the right attitude (the one described above is recommended).

The first tip in compiling your file of legal fake IDs is to keep your eyes open for anything that looks or feels official, anything that you can slap a date of birth on.

I took the ACT for this kid who worked at a rectory. He used to answer phones for the priest and nuns.

If you're thinking what I'm thinking, you're right. Priests don't get too many calls, according to him. He said they got maybe one or two calls during his four-hour shift. They had shifts! Like they were really worried about getting those one or two calls. And he barely answered those. He'd turn on the answering machine, run around the place looking through stuff, and come back and just play back the answering machine, copy the message and leave it for the Father on his desk (they had desks!). Anyway, this guy wanted me to take the ACT for him, but didn't have much money. And really, if I got caught, I figured it'd be easier to get out of trouble, or at least not advance to another level of trouble, if we said I did it for free, as a favor but not for money. And I could lie and say I didn't do it for money, but you never know about the other kid. So it's best to not do it for money when you do it.

What he offered me instead was birth certificates. And he had access to the papal seal, well, an official Archdiocese of Chicago seal. The possibilities were endless. So we had a deal.

Now in order to take the test, I had to have two pieces of identification, which is what I'm talking about in the first place.

And there are many ways to do this. He gave me his social security card—the real American Express Card. He also had to let go fifteen bucks for me to go downtown to ID row and pick out some passport photo joint that also made IDs. Some of them are real smart and have this background that looks like the state ID and license background. They usually put on this show that you have to have three pieces of ID, one a license, one a social security card, and one other thing, but you can usually bring them around by saying the guy down the block likes your papers, but you like this place's background. If you got the ready cash, they'll take anything. Of course, this time I was set, with two hot pieces of ID: the social security card and the birth certificate.

Of course, keeping this new ID was also part of the favor he was doing for my favor. I couldn't slap a date of birth on it because saying I was born when he was born would do me no good with a bouncer, and jacking up his age would make him too old to be in high school for the ACT. So I made it a straight ID, with my picture on it and his name. I like to have lots of IDs anyway.

And this kid was good. He'd signed up for the ACT way before the test date, but even before he'd sealed his little application, he never had any intention of showing up for the test. He photocopied his information, including this little section in a box where you had to handwrite some kind of oath. He wrote big and sloppy, so it would be easy for his stand-in to forge. That's how much this guy planned ahead.

As far as his story goes, I got him a nice mid-level score. With his grades, he needed a "little" push to get him into college, not a bad college, but not great. But college is a good tie-in to the next family of IDs—college IDs.

One of my friends graduated early and was going to a really nice college. (The sad part of this story, which I don't want to get into, is that he got killed in a riot on campus, a riot which, you can guess, he started.) He had a part-time job working at the information desk which coincidentally dispensed the school's IDs. Students would take their social security card and registration card to the third floor of the building and show it to the secretary who would type up their names and social security number on a piece of paper, and slip it into this plastic card that had a blank space for a picture—which my buddy would take with this Polaroid-type machine at his desk. And then it was up to him to laminate it. And laminate we did. I would type up names I liked, dates of births I loved, and have picture after picture of me taken.

This was the same school that would buy back its used books at the back of the bookstore, so that on the way to the buy-back table, you could grab a few books off the shelves and sell them back new books you haven't bought.

I couldn't wait to get into college.

You could open a lot of doors with a birth certificate, a college ID, and another photo ID. Think of the new you, your fantasy career, the new place you were born, your real parents, get a feel for your new name.

Most criminals pick aliases very close to their legal names. Sometimes they even use their same first name. You are not a common criminal. Pick a completely different name. One you always liked, one you always wanted, one that sounds cool. Practice answering to it. That's the main reason people stick so close to their original name. You can baptize yourself with any name you want. Write letters to yourself using your new name. Save 'em so you'll remember who you are. Get to know yourself a little better.

Combined with the right presence, these papers can get you into most places. And after a few weekends, you'll know where your IDs will or won't work. You'll recognize the hardcore bouncers; others will just wave at you and let you in.

But if you want to have an easier time, or if you don't have the patience, the luck or the balls to try these first methods, and you have enough friends over twenty-one (I mean good friends) or you got some money to spend (how much is hard to say) then you gotta *really* break the law, kid.

I was born in '68. So what some of us were doing was buying white chalk pencils from art stores and dotting out the left half of the "8" in "68" on our licenses. All of a sudden we were five years older. Now in Chicago at the time, there was a system to your license number. Basically it was this 12-character number with a dash after each four characters. The first two sets of numbers started with letters, which were your initials, and ended with the numbers from your date of birth. So you had to make sure to blot out that "8" in your license number too or you were busted 'cause most bouncers knew that the "63" on your DOB should correspond to a "6" and a "3" in your license number.

Of course after too many of us descended on clubs all over town, a lot of bouncers started casually wiping their fingers across our pretty pictures, sending us back five years. (In fact, after I actually turned 21, the state started printing in huge red letters "UNDER 21" all around the borders of your license.)

So we had to come back with the ultimate weapon.

You will need to borrow from someone who is over twenty-one, but not too much older, you will need to borrow his birth certificate and social security card. He should have the same color hair, eyes, a height and weight similar to you. You'll also need a photo ID, which you already know how to get. The borrowee might charge you some bucks. Pay it. It's a risk on this person's part, and it's valuable to you. Of course, he might want a favor instead.

If you have a brother, it's not always the best idea to use his papers. First of all, he'll be looking over your shoulder all the time. Secondly, someday he might come to his senses and try to confiscate his name, social security number, and date-of-birth from your image. Thirdly, if he gets in some kind of trouble, and if you live in the same house, then trouble comes looking for you. Fourthly, this transaction is bound to come out someway or somehow, like over the dinner table or over an after-dinner argument. In the worst case you might wind up having to do your brother A FAVOR IN RETURN. This is the person who knows all about your childhood, knows the kind of scrapes you've been in, knows what you hate to do. The moral of this passage is this: You should not know too well whose brother you become. This will limit the person you can be.

Now take the borrowed documents to the proper state agency. I went right for the State of Illinois Center downtown. Present these documents, pay your fee, fill out the forms and you'll be given a license. A real license.

The tricky part is that you are not dealing with bouncers or passport photo dealers. You are messing directly with the state. You are breaking the law in order to continue breaking the law. Be very careful. Rehearse your part. Memorize every bit of information on the cards and any information stemming from it. Know what astrological sign you are. Know when the last time was that this person got a license or state ID and at which location. This is all on record. But don't be scared. As long as you know your story, as long as you have your papers, you are who you say you are.

But there's a catch once you've got your new ID.

Even if you paid to borrow this person's papers, even if he didn't think it was a big deal, even if you don't really like this person, you two are now linked. Even if it's in a small way, you two are now linked.

You'll more than walk in this person's shoes. You'll turn around when someone calls his name. You'll be able to drive to the store as this person. You'll know what it's like to be a Gemini even if this wasn't your original birth sign.

And he'll know that somewhere out there is someone that can assume his identity at any time. And he will think of this from time to time, after it's too late.

You owe it to this person to take care of yourself, to not screw him over. If you get a ticket with this person's license, it'll go on his record. If you fuck with the cops and are thrown in jail and present this license as your identity, the arrest will go on that person's record. If there's a warrant for your arrest, that person might find himself surrounded by cops. If you're caught with two licenses with two different identities, you're both fucked. Take care of your other half. Remember, when it comes down to it, this is a battle between you and the state. Your friend is just trying to help.

There is a lot of responsibility that goes with this act. But hey, you're twenty-one now, and you should start acting your age.

So good luck, have fun, be careful, and welcome to the club.

H U N G R Y

I wake up naked next to Jester's naked girlfriend, and I'm scared. Any second he might walk in, pause, whip out a shotgun and give me the ax.

My clothes are just below the bed, an arm's reach away, so I reach. My pants are dry now. My shirt smells like an old towel, but I don't give a shit. That thin bit of fabric can at least kind of slow down the bullet. It's better than being shot naked. And Farah doesn't look quite as gorgeous as she did the first time I saw her, or all of those times I flipped off thinking about her.

Laying there, not posing, just like she was flung on the bed, lines from the sheets on her face, her arm bent in a way it doesn't seem it should be able to go, her palm kind of facing up with her elbow turned down, no makeup, Farah looks just pretty.

I want to wake her up.

But I don't know whether I could kiss her.

I slowly pull off my cover and try not to shake the bed as I wiggle back into my stale pants, my coarse shirt, grope for my shoes.

Maybe she'd been drunk last night. Maybe she was really

expecting Jester. I would've liked to have had more sex with her, but I wouldn't even know how to bring it up. "So, are we boyfriend and girlfriend now? I really enjoyed that. Did you? Don't answer that. When can we meet again? Do you like me more than you like Jester?" What if she tried to tell Jester I raped her? What if she told him that I came in my pants?

I kiss her on the cheek. It's warm. The room smells sticky, is bright with sunlight, like we're in a spotlight.

The floor is cold. I'm a little woozy. I'm hungry. I have a sex hangover: like a tight hat on my head. My eyes so dry I feel every millimeter of my eyelid as it passes over my eyeball for a blink, and my mouth is dry. The booze and the sex. And I'm about to get shot.

My feet stick to the floor as I tiptoe out of the bedroom. (Fuck my socks.)

On the way to the living room door, I pick up the receiver to her telephone and memorize her phone number from the little white slip that it's written on.

Outside, Winter is sliding away. The cement's dark from a light drizzle which with a slightly colder breeze would've been a light snow. It's a nice cold, and it does a better job than caffeine. And I'm happy 'cause Jester is not in shooting range. But there's a parking ticket shoved under the wipers. Busted— for parking in a residential area without a parking permit. In this neighborhood, Lincoln Park, the folks had enough money to lobby for this type of law, to pay metermaids to enforce it. So though Jester may not have known what I'd done, the neighbors were out patrolling on a Saturday night, making sure outsiders paid for parking their asses where they didn't belong. And to think I'd always thought it would be a big shit deal to shit in your own Lincoln Park, Northside Brownstone shitter.

I jump in my car, grab my three-quarters length coat from the back seat, and drape it over my legs and stomach, like an old caveman animal skin.

I pulled on to Halsted and drove south, and this city is laid out in a straight line for me. I drive in the direction that the real estate values dropped, past what was The University of Illinois at Chicago which devoured Maxwell Street, which I can't look up in a history book while I'm alive, which will appear on a CD-Rom after I've passed away.

Movies and TV shows are always too short to show this

part of the deal, the long half-hour drive home, grilling myself.

Did I just screw a friend over? Or did I add a turn of the screw to the turn of the screw? Was Jester behind this? Was he manipulating me, tricking me into having sex with his beautiful girlfriend? That fiend. Or was Farah just that bad?

On TV you don't wind up driving behind a bus. If you do, the sign on back has to be an ad for gym shoes telling me to "Just Do It," telling anyone who glimpses to just do it. The sign in front of me is for a generic brand of cigarettes.

And the bus is slowing me down.

I wonder how many people can tell that the night before I had sex with a gorgeous woman who was using me for my talent. Going this slow, maybe a few people can look through my window and catch a glance and maybe a glimpse of my sign.

It's a bunch of red lights, missed car accidents, a-thousand-dollar-per-block-drop-in-property-value.

In front of my house is parked the Hernandezes' station wagon. It's Sunday. I missed Church. Inside, I'm sure the menudo is being poured into gaudy, flowered dishes with chips in the side. Chips that've been dyed red from years and years of menudo passing over that chip. Dishes with hair line fractures, thin black lines passing through the bouquets that despite all the menudo, all that pig stomach, hominy, red chili, despite all that, the flowers on the dishes have not grown nor wilted. Dishes served on a kitchen table that looks like a bridge table that anyone who played bridge would not play bridge on because of its gold flecks and curly blue flowers in the corner and its steel, skinny legs.

I don't know why I go home. Because...it was time to leave Farah's house. I'm hungry. I am starving. My stomach is flapping its lips, and I want to eat good food.

I grip the steering wheel harder, pulling it into me like I'm fucking it.

I go home because I'm hungry.

KILL ME, JESUS

I stepped inside the house.

My mother, a bright green apron over the purple flowered Church dress, was walking through the hallway. She held up her hand as I opened my mouth. She stepped to the picture shelves near the door, stuck her other hand behind some picture frames and pulled out three packs of paper-wrapped *Milagro* tortillas. She shoved them into my chest and whispered in Spanish, *"You just brought these back from the store."* They were cold.

What would I do without all these wonderful women lying for me and to me?

I whirled around, caught a whiff of the tortillas wet corn husk smell, caught a whiff of my dad and my someday-to-be-father-in-law in the kitchen arguing about soccer teams, walked back outside, tortillas against my chest.

Outside once again, the cold seeped into me. I watched my breath.

Things were serious enough inside that my mom thought she had to give me a really good excuse for not going to Church in the morning and for not being there when they all got back to eat and for God knows what else.

95

The cold tortillas felt shrivelled as I back-tracked to my car, reopened my car door and slammed it.

I prayed that I wouldn't spend my entire life smuggling tortillas and trying to find out if I'm married or not.

I rubbed the food on my chest, under my coat, hoping to heat them up. Inside I would have to keep my big, incriminating mouth shut until I figured out was going on. To muster the patience, I had to first slow down my re-entrance and take a little time to imagine Rosie bawling in the cab, Rosie trying to tell the fat, smelly, unshaven, but kind-hearted cab driver where she lived.

Of course this didn't sound like the Rosie I knew, but I wasn't the guy she used to know. Maybe I had pushed her to tears. But not that dramatically. Was I that important? Did I change that much?

I felt giddy wondering if she reacted the way I thought, like I was waiting to find out how some audition went, like I wanted to hear, but didn't want to hear, like the truth would not make me out to be as important as I wanted to be. And it was like coming with Farah was just a dream. I couldn't exactly remember how good it felt. All I had was the soreness in my stomach muscles, the cotton in my head, a tired body and sore dick.

For this entrance, Rosie was walking through the hallway. She spotted me. She didn't look mad. She looked unmovable, confident, as if I was the one who was abandoned last night, which I guessed, in a way, I was, but technically I had chased her out. So I thought I had the power. Until a few facts crystallized in my head: 1) If I asked Rosie if she had cried in the cab, she would've laughed in my face; 2) My mom really, really, really wanted to cover-up my late night out; 3) I had no idea what I was walking into.

I started to think that maybe it would've been nice to have been bored with them at Church, for my knees to start hurting halfway through the Our Father (the first of three prayers we kneel through), to hear people try to sing together, to eavesdrop on what people are talking about when they're supposed to be praying.

So she stood there looking confident, actually pretty sexy: a skirt, white stockings, a blouse with a tight red T-shirt underneath, and I knew how hot she looked through that tight shirt, her nipples poking through. And I stood there, shifting a manhandled pack of tortillas from one hand to the other, staring at the wall between me and the kitchen like I'm trying to figure out how high it is. And my old man was laughing his ass off over something her old man just said.

"You owe me twenty bucks for a cab ride," Rosie said.

"Why did you leave?"

"You aren't serious."

"Yeah."

"You owe me twenty bucks."

"I'll have it next Friday."

"You also owe me another hundred."

"Heh, heh, heh," I said, pronouncing each "H."

She handed me a blue ring box. "This is the ring you're giving me. I put it on layaway." She didn't blink or pause when she said this because there was no proof on earth to the contrary.

"Did you cry in the cab?" And I gotta ask this. "I" would never ask such a dorky question, but my persona is confused and unsure at the moment and hers is strong. And the only reason I did ask was because she seemed so strong, so mean, so mad, so calculating that I suspected that maybe last night she just drove to some other place to party to teach me a lesson. So I gotta be dorky enough to see if she just didn't laugh wickedly.

"And I thought you were only *acting* stupid," is all she said.

I grabbed the ringbox and walked into the kitchen, ready to act too outlaw to be an in-law. I accepted her challenge because I felt I could beat her at my own game and because I'd hardly seen this side of her, her acting like it was her game. It turned me on. I thought maybe we *could* be together—if I beat her at my game or we tied at our game. If she won, fuck no. I wasn't about to marry a woman like that.

I walked into the kitchen. My dad squat next to her squatter dad, next to Rosie's leather-skinned mom. My mom's chair was empty. She served everyone so that she could make sure I had an excuse. Rosie's chair was next to my electric chair.

"Buenos días," I said, as I put the tortillas in the middle of the table. They quieted down as I, the largest of their sperm and eggs, walked into the kitchen my dad bought and my mom decorated.

I was bigger than them. I'd gotten further in school than

all of 'em. If I based it on test scores, like the outside world did, they'd say I'm smarter, too. So what did it mean? It meant I was late for breakfast, so they had to wash out a dirty menudo dish to pour my pig stomach and hominy soup into.

"If I had a son, Don Manuel," Mr. Hernandez said, "I wish he would have the decency to wake up, not say anything to anyone, and instead get the tortillas for us. I was about to die from lack of flour."

"They make them out of wheat now, Don Garrafino" my dad added. "Wheat!"

"Let me guess, Don Manuel, on the north side."

"Goat's cheese quesadillas!"

"Barbaric. What blasphemy is next? Sheep's brain-lite? Low-fat cow tongue? There's nothing sacred anymore."

"We must have used up sacredness, so the world is coming to an end. The Spanish conquest is coming to an end. It's the violent end of the sixth sun."

"But the sun never sets on the Americans' conquest."

Mr. Hernandez grabbed the tortillas. "And if I had a son, I would want him to go as far as he had to to get the best tortillas, even if it meant they got a little cold." He turned to his wife. "*Cariño*, heat these up for me." He turned back. His wife rose to heat. "The tortillas must be very good. They feel as if you went quite a ways away. I thank you, son."

"He's brought them back practically frozen before."

"You've done an excellent job of teaching him, Don Manuel."

"It's impossible not to teach him something."

"*¡Mujer!*" Then Mister Hernandez gave his wife a Mexican shout, one exclamation mark upside down, another right side up. "Don't go near the microwave. I want them naturally heated." She kept walking and slightly altered her path so that she wound up in front of the stove instead of the micro, as if that was what she was walking toward in the first place regardless of what her initial trajectory seemed like.

"This womens liberation has gone too far. I don't mind store-bought tortillas every other week, but I can't stand the microwave. Melted cheese, melted tortillas, melted plastic cups, I can't stand it." He sucked some menudo off his spoon. My dad watched him and took that moment to eat, too. "I told the girl, Rosie, I said to her..." Hernandez reminded us of his girl's name because he cheated on her, too. We all cheated on

Rosie. "Rosie, computers are the future, but computerized tortillas, well, that's the limit."

Mrs. Hernandez returned with the tortillas hot with new dark spots from the sizzling griddle.

These men were smart, too.

They had a way figured out to make the ladies stretch out the life spans of the menudo dishes and revive the cold tortillas. And I liked not washing the dishes, and it was nice to have the chopped cactus and the sheep's brain brought to me. And I wish I'd killed the pig that we were about to receive. "Here, Daddy," I wish this young warrior could have said, "I've saved the pig's balls for you."

"¡Mujer!" This was Hernandez again with the double exclamation mark shout. "Let Rosie serve the boy." She'd made the mistake of coming back with my bowl of menudo.

Rosie stood as her father opened his mouth, had my bowl in her hands as her father finished saying "boy." She poured my bowl back into the pot, stirred the pot, stirring and watching the mix in the silence.

She poured from the hot, steel, silver pot and fiddled around with the dishes near the pot.

I got a bowl with the hot, red stew, with jalapeños floating in it, sticking their heads out of the surface like crocodiles. And she knew I didn't eat even green M&Ms 'cause they remind me of the hot shit. She knew I didn't eat the hot shit, and her folks as well as my folks gave me shit for not eating the hot shit.

Everyone watched. I was supposed to answer in a cute way, say something clever for her to get them out of there and serve me the right way, but too much was at stake with this pig guts soup. "Look at this," I listened to myself say out loud. "Why did she put all this hot shit in my menudo? She knows I hate hot shit. Look at all this hot shit." I grabbed a fat jalapeño by the tail and showed them the size of it to make my point.

"I won't have that kind of English at the table, son. Apologize to Mr. Hernandez."

"Mr. Hernandez," I recited, "I apologize for my indiscretions. But your daughter knew I was hungry. She had been asked to serve me. She knows I hate chili, and still she gives me a bowl full of jalapeños." I let the fat prop plop into the bowl. "She is unfit."

"Son, son, son," and it seemed bizarre for these words to

come out of Mr. Hernandez as he looked at me, "son, she is very fit. You simply need to know how to talk to her. She doesn't know your language yet. Daughter, Sweetie, fix your future husband's menudo for him the way he likes it."

She did not say a word. She picked up the bowl, carried it to the sink and dumped it. She went to mix and fiddle with the pots again.

"Well, I'm glad the issue came up, Rosendo," Mr. Hernandez said. "We have much to discuss."

"Many, many, many details," my dad added.

Both dads gulped menudo and watched each other as they jiggled their full jowls as if they were communicating something to each other.

"Rosie has never had a boyfriend before," Father Hernandez said, which I know was not true. She WAS a virgin until she met me, but she'd had many a boyfriend when she was supposed to be at rehearsal for a sweet-fifteen, at a school function, registering voters for elections. "How many girlfriends have you had?" Everyone stopped eating and stared at me as if they'd rehearsed this some evening while I was out.

"Twenty."

"Twenty?" Old "H" said. "I suppose that will have to do. Though it would be better if the man had more experience than that. One-and-a-half to two per year is a respectable average."

Right over my shoulder, like a bullet just hissing by, the steam and just the tiniest hot edge of the menudo dish was shoved over my shoulder, past my face and in front of me. This girl was tough. The only easy test with her would be the blood test.

"There are things a really affectionate father requires for his daughter," Hernandez said.

I let the menudo sit while he speechified. Rosie was somewhere behind me, I wished, standing behind me waiting for my approval, but I knew better.

"Do you drink?"

"Don Garrafino!" my dad said. "The boy is only eighteen."

"Oh, is he too young to speak for himself?"

"No," I replied. "I'm old enough to put my own foot in my mouth."

"You have to be very young to be that flexible. When you get old, when you get married, it will always be someone else's. Now, son, do you drink?"

I didn't look at my dad. I hoped he thought I was joking. "Yes."

"Good. I like a man who knows how to carry on in social situations. Don Manuel, I think you did a good job in giving him his morals. But I can see that the Americans slipped some in, too. It's a shame he hasn't learned how to twist them. Is the boy bright?"

"You should hear some of his excuses, Don Garrafino. He's very bright. He'll be in college next year."

"We don't have any college boys in our family. We were all too smart for school. We learned everything we needed right away. But I suppose nowadays things have to be explained longer, so good. We'll marry into a college boy. He won't work for four years, but when he finally does, he can make up all that salary in eight years. In the mean time, Don Manuel, I am confident that you will provide ample support for my daughter. When should she move in?

"But nothing's been settled, Don Garrafino. There are procedures, customs, tricks."

"Of course, of course, I was simply testing. Does the boy speak Spanish?"

"Don Garrafino! You've known my son for years."

"Don't translate for him. Answer me in Spanish, boy."

"*Sí.*"

"Not at the table. The menudo's enough for now. There are certain things I will have to discuss that I can discuss in only English, though I won't go into indiscretions, but the wedding itself will be conducted in Spanish only. We must have the more moral language at the more moral component. Besides, I don't know how to say 'prenuptial agreement' in Spanish."

"Don Garrafino! We don't expect Rosie to sign a prenuptial agreement."

"No, I want the boy to. If he's going to be a student the rest of his life, and my Rosie is going to become his Rosie and is going to become a hard worker as I've instructed her—computers are very big you know—well then, she is going to save a lot of money, especially living under your roof and working—the boy will have to buy his own school supplies, really that is not a woman's duty. Clothes, food, something to drink, that's different. Those are things they can share with us, but books are selfish—therefore I want to protect our investment.

If Rosie makes all that money, and your son decides to leave her, he should not get her money. In fact, the American custom is for HER to get HIS money. That custom, of course, will not apply since your son does not work."

"But I do work."

My dad spit out some pig's gristle. "You work!" My dad said with a look he must have practiced for that very day, for that very moment.

Mr. Hernandez laughed and laughed at my dad's buggin' eyes, the way his tongue and the gristle shot out his mouth. "I love it...(he was still laughing at my dad) 'You work!'...ho, ho, ho, (He laughed exactly like that, magnified the giggles by shaping his lips in an "O" and pushing out air.) 'You work!' I love it." He patted me on the back. "That's wonderful. As long as you're not a mariachi or a comedian, I love it."

"But, Don Garrafino!" my dad answered. "He is."

"Oh my God! I didn't know he played the guitar."

"I don't. I'm a comedian."

"Rosendo," Mrs. Hernandez said, "I didn't know you were funny." And she got the biggest laugh of the day, maybe the week. No, I won't go a month. Not a month. But that was as hard as a group of people that size, of that weight, height, energy, that was as much as they were capable of laughing. It was the whole thing. And something like that, when it is or isn't for you, that's the time to stop. You can't get back up there if you try. And there are maybe one or two things you can say at that moment, but the phrases were being used by someone speaking Hindi in Australia and some drunken Cantonese dude telling dirty jokes somewhere in the Sudan. So I just shut up. Even right now I'm trying to be stupid silly, and other days when I'm bored or just letting my brain loose, I go back to that day and try to think of shit I could've said to win the audience but I can't. So I had to just let go of them. You need to do that sometimes.

And it wasn't really fair. I've never seen her mother naked, yet she'd fucked me, too. And if the father was that loud and stupid, and Rosie was so smart and sly, that meant the mother, oh the mother, she must have had it all figured out. She must have been the master-mind of master-minds, able to get her will by the glint of a plate, the temperature of a tortilla, the wisp of a hint or doubt, the setting of the lighting, and the well-placed argument. It would be different if they had a son.

A son will slow the woman down. That will keep the woman busy enough to become a mere genius. With no break from men, she could not become an evil genius. Which meant Rose had been taught all the tricks. And Rosie was good. She'd fucked me more times than I'd fucked her. And at least I did it when no one was around. And at least I warned her by letting her take off her clothes, by taking off mine. At least she knew when it was going to happen. Me, whenever she was around, and I got clothes on—I could get fucked, what with this mom giving her all the tricks. And even though I thought I was at my strongest, Rosie was actually at her most powerful, not her meanest, I don't think. I think she loved me so much she wanted to do some bizarre, motherly tough-love thing; nonetheless, she was strong, and I had a feeling that even when she wasn't around, and I was wearing clothes, she was fucking me.

So the only way to win was for me to keep my clothes off as much as possible.

I had time to think all this and a little more as I slopped up my tepid menudo, waiting for the last laughs to dribble out like a weak piss.

My menudo was cold I decided. I tried to spoon an island of floating red chili sauce, tried to scoop a little pool of oil from the red murky water. I made them quiet with my silence and my spooning. When it was finally quiet, I said, "Rosie, this is cold now." I placed the spoon in the bowl, it slid underwater. I pushed the bowl away from me, "Heat this up for your future husband the way he likes it."

Before I'm done saying "it," her arm passed over my pistol-whipped cheek and passed back, bowl in hand. She was standing somewhere behind me. She ran to the sink, overturned the bowl to dump, set the flame on high, stirred the pot so we could hear the ladle hitting the sides. Again, this was louder than anything that day. It sounded like a fucking gong. And again I was fucked, like she had a pot over my head and was banging the shit out of it. She splashed hot menudo into my bowl, it splashed over the sides, onto her hands, the red juice dripped over her wrists with her still ladling. She turned.

Rosie pointed the bowl at me as if it could fire. "Don't I get a say in this? Don't I get a say?" She opened her hand and dropped my dish. It fell so straight and fast I thought it would bore a hole in the floor.

I didn't hear the smash.

Menudo covered the linoleum. It looked like she'd spilled her guts and inside was thin red water with chunks of gristled meat and white hominy chunks. The green specks of cilantro floating on top made the skin on one side of my face crawl.

"And don't I get a say," I said. "I get the last say. There is not going to be any wedding. I refuse to marry an unfit, clumsy, sneaky girl." I pulled out her ring box and tossed it in the puddle of menudo.

"Shut up, son. Stop it! I order you to stop it!"

"I'm sick of all this sneaky shit. I want to have it out right here. I want to tell the truth, I want to speak like a man."

"Don't raise your voice to me, boy," Hernandez stood up.

I got up and was a full six inches taller and forty pounds stronger. "I'll say what I have to say as loud as I have to say it, old man."

My dad got up as big as the house. Not an inch larger or smaller. He was as big as the house. Him I couldn't hit. He grabbed me by the shirt. "You apologize to these people. You get on your knees in the shit you spilled and apologize to these people or you get out of this house."

I looked at my dad. His dark eyes focused on me. His hand grabbing my shirt. I forget where everyone else was standing. "I guess I'll go, Dad."

Again with the rehearsed-surprised look on his face. He let go of me like I was too hot, opened his mouth wide, but did not say anything.

I turned to leave.

"Son." He didn't sound as hard now. "If you leave now, you can't come back." And he said this gently, like it was just some sad truth.

I shook my head. And I left.

Sometimes I don't believe I do the things I do, that I'm the one who's done the things I've done. I can separate myself from it.

Only Juan could be so smooth on stage. I can't believe Arterio is so down with the ladies. I love to watch him work. Marquez is such an ass to the teachers at school.

I know this must be a sign of psychosis, like I'm schizo. But I like to think that I've cultivated my schizophrenia.

It was only Rosendo who could sit at that table with the Hernandezes and address the mess that Juan'd got us into. It was only Rosendo who could leave like that. And I felt a little sad, but only as if I'd watched some melodrama on TV. For the rest of me, it would take some time for this to sink in.

We were all used to not being home at night, late, used to waking up early only to get out of the house to pretend I was going to school. Waking up and not having to pretend, that would be a shock to my system. It would not be until Monday morning that the rest of me would feel the real impact, get word of what Rosendo had done and would feel sad, genuinely sad to realize it was true.

You can drop me off in the middle of any city in the U.S. with just what I got in my pocket, and I can work my way to the top.

I was out to hook up with me, myself, and I, and call on Lorenzo Cassanova to give us a hand, see if Arterio had what it takes.

I had twenty bucks. My car. A $300 check coming next Friday, and a topless dancer for a girlfriend.

Drop me off anywhere in the U.S. with my car, the promise of 300 bucks, and a topless dancer, and I can work my way to the top.

JETHRO

If I had theme music, it would be playing right now, and while that Mexican-New-Wave-Punk-Rock-Psychedelic dittie seeped into your living room through surround-sound, my image would be goofily dancing around, a sort of hip-hop-cha-cha-cha-hat-dance, while I, the narrator, gave you the scoop about the incident that led me to being important, interesting enough to be broadcast.

But this not the story of a man named Brady. I don't want to tell ya' a story about a man named Jed. This is the tale of a cast away who's here for a long, long time.

Switched at birth by Basque acrobats who were fired from Monty Python's Flying Circus after they were caught sniffing glue without inviting the cross-dressing ringmaster with the termite infested wooden leg.

To the tune of "Allá en el Rancho Grande:"

This is the story of Tuburcio Sandoval, a gold prospector who was sitting on a gold mine but didn't know it. Everyday he would pan for gold in the main stream where there were so many miners along the bank, so many hungry prospectors sifting through the sediment, their fingers numb from the cold water, too numb to feel the tiny bits of gold that slipped into their pans. Until one day, a miner named Jester gave him a video recorder, and Tuburcio left it on at home overnight. When he went to work at the stream the next day, he took the recorder with him to film some exciting footage of people who've struck it rich. Instead, one of his workers popped out the video and slipped it into a player and saw Tuburcio's crazy parents...Mom—Alicia Sandoval—pretending not to know how to speak English but actually being fluent since she was three years old, pretending to be subservient to Dad but really, in the end, doing exactly what she wants and putting the family through exciting adventures with her wacky get-rich-quick schemes. (She makes a goofy face into the camera.)...Dad— Tuburcio Sandoval Sr.—illegal alien abandoned by Gypsy Basques who had to decide between lugging him around or lugging twenty pounds of bread. They really liked bread. He gives fencing lessons at the YMCA and likes to challenge neighbors to duels...Girlfriend—Rosie—blowing a wiener from the wrong end—and the audience eats it up...Jester—as bald as a shaved testicle and full of as much shit as an ass—and laughs and laughs...and Farah—gorgeous, make-the-Skipper-Professor-and-Gilligan-fight-over-her-gorgeous.

Tuburcio told the audience of miners that he staged it all and unless they gave him some gold he wouldn't show them any more pictures of his family...er...his "TV Family," so they worked all the more harder to get more gold. He was like a fuckin' Aztec Prince, he had so much gold. All he had to do was put into practice his skills of panning, but now instead of a crowded stream, he's the only nut in these waters.

Tuburcio got as rich as a Beverly Hillbilly and as smooth as Jethro Bodine. Who the fuck is Jethro? You don't know who Jethro is? You must'a been born too late to know what an 8-track looks like, or you must'a been born before the days when you had to declare a major in grammar school.

Jethro went from black and white to color TV. Jethro went from hunting in the hills of Tennessee to hunting in Beverly— Hills, that is. Jethro went from being one of the boys in the woods, a tough bastard, smart as the guy next to him, knew a sick possum from a brilliant thespian possum, went from a smart poor fuck to a rich fuck, a rich stupid son-of-a...son of a what? Who was Jethro's mom, dad? Why did he live with his uncle and granny? That question and more on the next "Geraldo," with guest psychiatrist Bob Newhart.

Oil riched-up uncle, Jed, Jed Clampitt, Jethro's guardian, legal guardian? Probably not. But we can assume, knowing the simple, wholesome ways of these folks, that Uncle Jed was more family than the court or state could ever summon for someone.

Jethro tried to buy Canada. Tried to become a G-Man. Almost played for the Dodgers. Tried to do stand-up.

You really think you know Jethro.

I do.

Okay, so the Clampitts...they're this sweet little family who never really wanted anything more than to take care of their critters, eat their hog jowls, maybe square dance now and then, and then they got rich 'cause Uncle Jed, the patriarch, was hunting one day and shot at some game, missed (which was rare), hit the ground and oil squirted out of the ground, his ground. So they got rich, moved to Beverly Hills, and then the oil bust came and wiped them out. Only now they're worse off than when they started because they got a little used to some of the fancy city stuff (though they could really never catch on. It was kind of like traveling through time and going to the future, or another planet, and there's so much new shit and new technology that you don't get it.) and the folks back home read so much about them in the papers that they got a little jealous, thought the Clampitts thought they were so high up. Now the folks back home aren't so nice to them anymore. The folks back home don't want to have to keep up with the Clampitts.

So you think Jethro's gone.

You claim not to know Jethro.

We resurrected his image. Like Frankenstein, we had the right formula all along. We just didn't realize the right combination.

And we resurrected his image, one atom, one molecule, one pixel at a time.

First you couldn't run from Uncle Milty or Lawrence Welk. Ed Sullivan was a vampire.

But now we have television grottos to hide in, exclusive channels—country clubs of the air waves. We got TV ghettos—real programming crimes going down.

Jethro was once Prime Time. Prime Time once meant something. Everyone was programmed to watch the big shows after 7 p.m., after the family ate steak and potatoes.

The programmers said, "Screw you lazy mutherfuckers who watch TV at 3 in the morning. Forget you if you want news now." If you were a man at home at 1 in the afternoon, you were a girlie man and had to watch womens shows.

Jethro didn't like that shit. But he also got bored of his video library, though sometimes he'd have that running just so he could flip to a video of his choice if there wasn't anything good on any other channel of the world, or at least the colors of the video he picked added a nice tone to the television mosaic he'd create by flipping through channels, a pink tone, a skin color tone 'cause Jethro's watching pornos, American pornos.

Today, I don't care about your astrological sign, your social security number, tell me which channels you have programmed into your automatic flip pallet, and we'll know if we have something to talk about. We'll know if we can talk about underground, overground, really overground TV, which cable you've stolen.

Jethro bought a spaceship. He bought fuckin' NASA. He got a bionic arm and a bionic eye. And a bionic ear. And a bionic leg. And, since he likes pornos so much and he's got the money, he had the surgeons throw in a bionic cock.

So he's not that stupid. Is he?

Humans can live so long now that there are actually people who remember prime time, who remember "The Beverly Hillbillies" on prime time.

The TV syndicate thought they could buy and control Jethro. But even stupid mutherfuckers learn after a while. Year after year of making the same blunders, running and rerunning the same wacky miss-takes. Studying yourself in color and black and white. You wise up.

You thought he went away.

There was a time when you were an outcast if you didn't watch the right program—a Minnow stranded on an island, a fish out of water—at sea!

There weren't too many to pick from. Everyone was on the same program. Fuck you if you weren't. Then there were reruns, then more channels, more shows, then a flood of a flood of channels, a month of Sundays of programming to fill on any given Tuesday.

You saw Jethro as a baby. You saw him on syndication. Now we can see him on the '70s channel. You can be more

precise with the 1979 channel. First we had the Beverly Hillbilly Marathon—straight chronological broadcasts of every
episode, then it played and played, two shows a night.

Then we brought Jethro, not just back to life, but to life.

We were able to put him in new episodes by grafting from
the old footage. Jethro learned shit. It was an age of enlighten-
ment where we would not tolerate the old way. No stasis.
Characters would no longer have to wear the same clothes
season after season.

And Jethro learned Kung Fu. This is the man who could lift
logs, throw 150-mile-an-hour fast balls, hit a fly with a rock at
100 yards. And this was BEFORE he got his bionic parts. Fuckin'
right he was good at Kung Fu. And he learned how to Rap.

Jethro would assert himself a little more and a little more
with every episode which life brought him.

And he took all the Clampitts' money and, knowing what
he knew, invested around oil, diversified their financial port-
folio, invested in the media, got out when it got risky, got into
computers, and regenerated himself, again.

You can't cancel Jethro. You can't pluck him out of the
woods—mutherfucker—make him rich and then ice him. He's
out there. He's out of everyone's woods. You gave him the ax
and now he's swinging it, chopping down your door, fucking
up your cars, cutting your cable.

Don't run.

Y'all come back now, hear?

LUCKY TIO

Sunday is a slow night at the topless bar.

Farah goes to relax, she says, have some strapping young man buy her some drinks, make gas money, maybe enough for groceries. "Strapping" means rich or at least has money to blow.

The woman sitting behind the counter, in front of a digital cash register, didn't look like a dancer. She was in her forties and I was shocked that her rolls of fat didn't vibrate with the music from the club. She did have on the required three pounds of makeup and the gallon of perfume. She asked for my ID and I handed it over. "Ooooh. Lorenzo Cassanova. That's a sexy name."

"Thanks, Babe. Do I live up to it?"

She smiled, handed it back and looked at me. She nodded her head, "You'll do," she said. "That'll be five bucks, Sweetie."

"On a Sunday?"

"New policy on Sunday. It's five bucks unless you have a pass or you're a special guest."

"Well, I'm a special guest of Farah."

She looked over a list of names on a clipboard on the counter. "Sorry, there's no Farah here tonight. Is that her real name or her stage name?"

"Shit. That's her real name."

"What does she look like?"

"Blonde, good lookingʼ, big boobs..."

"You just described half the dancers that work here."

"She hangs out with a guy named Jester."

"Oh, you mean, Genie." She swiveled in her chair to hang the clipboard, and I could smell her potent perfume all over again. "Hey, Candice," she shouted. A cute, dark-haired waitress walked up to us. "Can you tell Genie that Lorenzo is here to see her?"

Of course, I couldn't say, "No, my real name is Tio." She wouldn't know who the fuck Lorenzo is. "I don't want to cause you any trouble," I said. "I'll just go in and look around." I gave her the five bucks.

"Do you want me to find you a table, Sweetie?" the waitress asked.

"No, that's fine, Honey. I'm just gonna look around."

The five bucks hurt, but I parted with it. I figured that even if Farah said she knew someone named Lorenzo, I'd have to explain to her why I needed a fake ID. And if I fucked up in the explaining, she might figure out my real age, and she might not be too thrilled to find out she was fucking a high-school senior, even an ex-high-school senior. And now I needed her.

I don't know how much older than me she was because whenever I asked how old she was, all she would say was, "Young." She looked about 23 or 25.

My eyes had to adjust to the dark. Besides a few shadows around me, all I could see was the stage, and TVs in the corners, TVs showing the woman on stage. She was a tall, redhead with small breasts wrapped in a tight, red band of cloth, dancing to some Bon Jovi song. I hate Bon Jovi. And I had to just kind of stand near what I could tell was an empty table, ʼcause it was so dark you might wind up sitting on a customer or knocking over some drinks.

Planet Men is small. Instead of seven continents it has only four stages, one main one with a thin pole in the middle that the redhead was holding as she swayed, and three smaller stages spread throughout the room. Instead of constellations, there were five televisions hanging from different parts of the ceiling, so that you did not have to strain your neck to feed your eyes, just in case you could not get a good look.

The farthest stage against the back of the place was the

only other stage holding up a woman. She had her butt in the air and was looking at us men from between her legs, her face lined up with her light green thong, her knockers hanging to her chin and stretching her green top.

My wiener started waking up, sore walls and all. Farah had savaged and screwed me real good the night before. But this was like the Playboy Channel coming to life. I'd never been in one of these places before. I'd heard of them and knew of them, but I also knew it cost you money to hang out here, lots of money. Which is something I didn't have, even when I had a home.

The song faded out, the deejay, in a booth to the right of the stage, said the girl's name was Desire, and she'd be taking her top off during the next song. Yes! And it was Van Halen. I like Van Halen. And Desire rocked. Her boobs were small but nice and pointy, firm. A guy walked up to the stage and stood there while she danced in front of him. She bent down and he stuck a buck in her G-string. She gave him a kiss.

I felt a hand on my shoulder. This gorgeous black-haired dancer leaned her side against me and asked, "Would you like some company, Sweetie?" "Yes," I thought. "Desperately." But I had to say that I was waiting for Genie. She said okay. And now I could see the whole place. Drooling had helped me see in the dark. There were round tables spread throughout the room, and booths against the walls. The place was maybe a quarter full, and here and there I could see women topless in front of a sitting man, flipping their long hair in some guy's face; a woman sliding down a man's chest, between his spread legs; a woman laying on the floor, opening and closing her legs, pulling at her G-string, just exposing the sides of her shaved box.

I slipped into an empty chair near the middle of the place because my boner was trying to burst through my pants and straining itself in the process. I had to sit so as to make a dome with my pants to give my pud some more room. The dancer on the far stage had really interesting knockers. They were medium but boasted these huge, dark brown areolas and pointy nipples. They must've kept the place cold to keep the dancers' nipples hard. An old white dude in some kind of golfing shirt and pants stood in front of the stage. He stuck a dollar bill down her G-string, she kissed him, than he stuck another. She laughed and gave him a bigger kiss, and he gave her another bill, she laughed, and stuck her hooters in his face. He pretended to faint. He whispered something in her ear, and she shook her head. He left the side of the stage.

When the song ended, the deejay said, "Put your hands together for Desire," and I'm surprised anyone clapped since he asked and most of the men had half-naked women in front of them. Some ladies hooted and I turned to see where they were. There were dancers lined up against the bar, and some were sitting at two tables in front of them. It was a slow night for them.

There was no sign of Farah.

A waitress came up to me and asked if everything was all right. I asked how much the beer was, and she told me that domestic was $4.75 and imported beer was $5.50. I tried not to yell "Holy Shit." But I did say that I would wait to order until my friend showed up. I bought some lunch earlier, and after the cover charge, I had only ten bucks left. So a beer would've been nice, but I was hoping Genie would appear and grant me a few wishes.

Planet Men. In that particular club, at that particular time, Planet White Men. Everywhere you turned was a white woman half-naked, a woman just waiting to objectify one of the white men with money. Use me and I'll use you. Objectify me and I'll objectify you.

"Gentlemen and Gentlemen," the deejay said, "at the top of stage, for your viewing pleasure, the exotic, the luscious, the I-can't-believe-she's-human-mega-babe, Genie."

And out came Farah in a red, white and blue striped G-string, a star-spangled top, and I was saluting. Smoke billowed out from somewhere on the ceiling, and red and green and white lights swirled around her as she walked on stage.

She was baaaad, dancing to Motley Crue's "Too Young To Fall in Love," coming out prancing, waving her arms up and down, stepping wide, bouncing. If it wasn't for the fact she was half-naked, she might've looked dorky. But she was bouncing, sending the stars representing the west coast for one serious quake. And quake, quake, quake. One hand on the pole in the middle of the stage she had, walking around it, running her hand up and down the pole, prancing. I had finally seen prancing. I thought I would die and never see someone really prance. She did a long-legged, toes skipping off the floor, but not high enough to be jumping, but enough to clickity-click the topless club's main stage floor—prancing. She was Prancer, and she could pull my sleigh any night.

And then boom—she falls into the splits!

Just falls, like she's taking her next step and then boom, she was legs-spread-on-the-floor, bopping to the guitar riff part, just like the musician imagined it when he wrote the riff, when he deedled it out on his Stratocaster. And the boys start lining up in front of the stage, even before she's taken off her top. And my baby's got all kinds of possible moves from the floor, spinning on to her ass, twining her legs in front of her, right and left, right and left, then back over her head, and she rocks forward, spreads her legs and pushes herself forward, shoves her face in front of the first fat, white guy in front of the stage. And I'm a little jealous when she kisses that Andy-Griffith's-Grandfather-lookin'-tall-fat-guy with thick glasses, in the baggy, gray pants of an office-slug. But then I think that it's okay 'cause he's gotta pay for what I get for free. And then she rolls to her left to the next tip. Let's just say Motley Crue didn't make the song long enough and mister deejay had to back the song up till the boys ran out of singles. But that was just the first round.

After the song died out, the deejay said, "There's more. Genie's coming back out one bra less." Then more Motley Crue, this time "Shout at the Devil," and there's Farah, just like I remembered. And she jumps onto the pole, grabs on with her hands over her head and hangs there for a second, then she spins around, her legs pointed in the air and clamped around the pole, just like I remembered. And she lets go of her hands and arches her back downward, slowly, letting her tits seemingly slide toward her face, like an ice-cream ava- lanche. And then she pulls herself up, hops off the pole and shakes for the fellas fighting to get close enough to give her a buck. But it's too easy to just waltz over and pluck 'em from their hands.

She slams into the splits, twirls her head into a hair tornado, rolls backwards, shoots her legs in the air, balancing on her shoulders, boobs over her face.

Just like I remembered.

And somehow, through some kind of steel will I didn't know I had, I kept my hands off my crotch, but it was hurtin', not just from fighting with my pants, but 'cause he knew what it was like to be in THERE, and all the visual cues and physical cues were telling him that he should be in there now, but from the dull, deep pain over my stomach, that deep, hot empty feeling, it knew it was summoned just to hurt, to strain against my pants.

She knocked off some middle-aged dude's glasses with a swipe of her tits.

After the main stage, she had to dance on the smaller stage and then they opened another stage for her. She danced to six songs in all. I was one of the last guys to tip her. Four quarters down the G-string, just to let her know I was here. She got a kick out of me getting a kick out of her. This was the twenty-minute workout I'd never seen, but always imagined Rosie doing.

Farah came to my table. She had a red satin dress stretched so tight over her star-spangled bikini that the lines from the bra and G-string bulged like fat veins. She plopped a pile of singles on the table and started counting and straightening them out. Not exactly the way a boyfriend expects to get greeted, but I figured older folks might do it differently, plus she'd probably laugh at the word "boyfriend."

She was breathing a little heavy, counting in short breaths, bouncing her head on each count. "Whew," she slouched and breathed out, "That's a lot for on-stage."

"Do I get a kiss or what?" I said.

She sat up, "I'm sorry, Sweetie." I didn't want to be called "Sweetie" anymore in that place. She gave me a two-dollar kiss. I was special.

Our waitress came by and asked if everything was all right. I'm getting kissed by a babe in front of a pile of money, and she asks me if everything's all right.

The singles made a fat stack 'cause the bills were wrinkled and there was air between 'em. I caught a whiff of it as I passed it to the waitress who stalled to rearrange her tray. Stinky money, like dough, which is where the name must've come from, like sourdough, and cigarettes, like someone just blew a quick puff in your face.

She laughed at the stack and counted it with her head bobbing, too. You counted money with your whole body in this joint. And then she handed Farah three crisp, bright white twenties, slippery against each other. Farah took off her white pump and stuck the money in her shoe, further monetary fragrance.

"Set me up with a Turkey shot, a Seven and Seven, and bring this handsome young man a Spanked Monkey." Farah hopped on my lap.

We talked about Jester, we talked about comedy, comedy clubs, we kissed. The drinks arrived. We talked about the topless club, we kissed.

She treated me just like she treated the other guys, except I didn't have to give her tips and she bought me a few drinks. I didn't know how to ask if I could live with her, just for a while.

"I know Jester hasn't paid you shit yet," she said, "but how much does he owe you?"

"Three c-notes, Baby."

"I guess he's fucking you, too. We'll take care of that later." And I figured she might get me gigs someplace else, maybe even there, though I knew I'd have to get an all new set of material for this place. I'd make it after all.

So I just ogled her now and then, touched her legs now and then, nodded my head when she talked, talked about comedy, Jester, comedy clubs, topless clubs. The booze evaporated. We ordered more drinks.

Then a dancer ran up to Farah, stuck her blonde head next to Farah's blonde head, like she was gonna whisper, then yelled, "The Fart Face is here!"

Farah did a spit take, spit her drink all over the table.

She laughed. "Here's some easy money, T-O. This guy gives you an extra tip if you let him sniff your ass while you dance for him, and even more if you fart in his face."

"I'm not dancing for any man," I told her, and she laughed.

"He's been asking for you, Genie."

"I'll be back in a bit, 'T'."

"Are you really gonna let him do that?"

"Sweetie," there was that word again, "this guy runs up a huge tab. And besides," she got off my knee and my boner, "every man will eventually kiss my ass."

I believed that too.

There was a lady with a large tummy on stage. She even wore a tight skirt, to accent it I figured. No way to hide it when you're about to strip, but I guessed someone in the joint was into it.

And these guys were into whatever they were into but could be public about only in a place like this, if they could get away with it. I guessed Planet Men was the only place they would try to get away with it. Like bankers, and lawyers, and construction workers, and plumbers these guys looked like. Someone's sons, brothers, husbands, dads, trying to get away with who knows what on someone's daughter, sister, wife, mother. About to get away with it on my kind-of-girlfriend. But I would kick someone's ass if he tried to sniff Rosie's farts (the thought of which made me laugh).

The bearer of the fart news had been standing by my table, looking around and then asked if she could sit with me. "Sure, Babe," I told her. "Any girlfriend of Genie's is a girlfriend of mine."

She sat. "Can I have sip of your drink?" I had a beer by then.

"Sure, Doll."

She grabbed the bottle but didn't put her lips against it. She tilted her head up and held it just a little over her mouth and let the beer fall in to her mouth. "This place is full of weirdos," she said, and put down my beer.

I asked her to tell me a weirdo story.

She laughed, shook her head and started grinning.

"You look like you're remembering a good one," I egged her on.

"Good isn't the right word."

"That's even better."

"I can't believe I'm telling this. Shit, I can't believe it happened to me."

"What, what?" She had me laughing already. She could've said her bra strap broke and I would've laughed my ass off.

"It was my first time dancing. Like my second dance, as a matter of fact, and I had to get drunk to do my first dance. So I was sitting down, feeling a little buzzed, you know. I was putting my top back on, and this guy slips the twenty down my G-string from the front. And as he's pulling his hand out, he sticks his finger in my belly button." She covered her face with her hands, and shook her head.

"Come on, come on, Sweetie, let it out."

"Well, then he asks me if I ever had my belly button licked. And I say 'sure.' I mean, hey, I'm into that. But then he says, 'I mean from the inside.' And I say 'What?' And he says, 'I want to cut you open from here to here and lick your belly button from the inside.'"

"What? Holy shit."

"I got sober real fast, and I got up, but he grabbed me by the arm. But I mean grabbed. I had bruises around my arm afterwards. It really hurt, so I start to scream. And this customer who I danced for first comes over to see what's up, and this guy punches him out with his free hand. I mean like blood splashing from his face when he lands. So now I'm screaming my head off."

"Crazy."

"And then the manager, the deejay, the doorman, the bartender, and some customers run over. And this guy still has me by the arm, and he goes to punch the manager, but the bartender punches him first, and then the deejay grabs his shoulder, and there's some kind of nerve to pinch to make him let go. There's one in your wrist too, right about here." She grabbed my arm to emphasize the point, but I asked her to stop teasing me and to tell me the story.

"So the guy lets go...."

"Was he a big guy?"

"He was huge. A white guy, like 6' 3", 6' 4", big neck, big. But the deejay punches him again and then grabs him from behind like this..." again she used me for an example and grabbed the back of my shirt collar, "and from his belt, picks him up, knocks his head into the door, and throws him down the stairs. Then he goes down, drags him back up and punches him again. By that time the cops showed up."

"Shit."

"Shit's right. The guy wound up in the psycho ward. I wanted to go back to waitressing after that."

"Why didn't you?"

"Well, the manager liked me. Told me that was a one-in-a-million kind of thing."

"Now wait a minute. How do you know this Fart Sniffer you just sent my Genie to isn't a psycho?"

"He's harmless. He's just rich and perverted."

"Well, I wanna make sure. Where are they sitting?"

"Upstairs in a booth on this side." She pointed. "Don't worry, she's fine."

"I know, but I would still like to see this to believe it. I'll be back, and you can tell me another weirdo story." I figured Farah was either getting her cornhole licked, her hind sight cut open, or maybe I knew the dude, like it was Wally Autruck, my dad, my brother, my son maybe.

And it was!

Right as I got to the top of the stairs and turned, I could see at the end of the wall in a booth under a pink light, I could see Farah bent over, her G-string thong stretched to the side, and a big-headed creature's profile moving between her ass cheeks, like he was talking into her asshole, the flaccid red dress over his shoulder and her star-spangled bra draped over his head.

I had to sit on the steps. I couldn't believe I'd won. I mean, you play and you play and you play, and even when you stop thinking about winning—you keep playing. The only reason you stop THINKING about winning is that you've thought about it so much that your mind gets numb to the thought. But every time you play, it's like thinking it all those times you used to. And you always wonder what you'll do if you win, you kid around thinking about it seriously, and then boom, now you've got to figure out what to do with the money. This had to be how my dad had felt when he got the check from Ed McMahon.

Fart Face even had on the old, light green suit coat he wore to school. He licked ladies' assholes in the same coat he gave us detentions in. I was actually dumbfounded, with my mouth open, forming the sounds for 'Aaaahhh' but not able to say it. I knew the song playing and recognized the final riffs. I sat up a little to look over the side of stairs to catch a last glimpse. Wally was sitting back, smiling, and Farah was still waving herself in the air.

He might have smelled a fart, but I smelled early graduation. With no homework. And a wonderful recommendation.

So I sat there. Of course no one asked me to move. I get in no one's way. I will it that I should sit there for a second or two on the steps on the second floor of a topless bar with my principal's face in my girlfriend's ass. I don't want anyone to ask me to move, so no one does. And when I stand to collect my prize, even Farah has gone down the other flight of stairs.

Wally was leaning on the railing of the balcony, watching the dancer on stage, and before when I'd seen him near stairs or a railing I always wanted to push him over, but not then. Now I wanted him to live.

He was looking the other way, so he couldn't see me even out of the corner of his eye, which is where I always was at school, but on the rail he was too busy drooling at the ladies to keep me from blindsiding him. Even if he caught a glimpse of me, he wouldn't think to recognize me in the dark, in a bar, with his face still stinking like shit.

I slipped into his booth. It was covered with crumpled white napkins that I was not about to touch, a half mug of beer, and an ashtray with a heap of cigarettes. Funny, I never figured him for a smoker.

I sat there on the couch-type seat that circled the table. It was lumpy. He even shook his elephant ass to the beat a few times, clapped when the lady was done dancing, hooted a few times and then turned around.

He did a double-take. I mean like a real double-take, like a cartoon, rolled his head, his eyes bugged out, "What the..." type of double-take.

"Have a beer, Wally," and I'd been waiting all my life to say that.

"What the fuck are you doin' in here?" He jumped into the seat, pushed the table and shook the whole couch. He reached over and grabbed me by the shirt. "What in the fuck are you doin' here?" There was white spit coming out of his beerhole mouth, and he tried to pull me closer.

He shocked the shit out of me. I had him figured for a businessman—at all times. I pulled away and said, "Just hangin' out, Mr. Autruck."

He pulled me back. "I oughta beat the shit out of you like I always dream of doin'." And he had part of my shirt rolled up in his fat fist and he was digging his knuckles into my chest, one-hundred pounds at a time. I never imagined our fantasies would cross.

"Hey, I didn't have to show myself to you. I figured we could make peace, come to a gentlemens agreement."

He thought about it, then let me go with a shove. "Fuck if I buy you a beer. You're the one who should be kissing my ass."

"Nice choice of words," I thought. "Yeah, I'll buy you a beer," I said. "That's what I always wanted. You know, a beer with one of the guys."

"Shut the fuck up." He swallowed his beer.

But I didn't want to be a chicken shit. I had the power. Even though he was big, I was still faster, and could probably kick his ass. And I had the dope on him. If I was gonna be anything in life, I figured I couldn't let this giant asshole intimidate me right when I had him by the balls. "My girlfriend Genie opened a tab for me."

He said "Ah" when he finished the beer, kept the mug near his mouth. "What's your game, you little shit?"

I slid out of the booth. "Stop calling me names, you Fuck. We ain't in school. And when we go back, I got some heavy shit on you, so you better get used to calling me by a different name, mutherfucker."

He made to get up, but I pushed on the table and pinned him by the solar plexus with the table digging in just over his gut. "I'll get your ass thrown in jail first, Wally. You better cool down." I wished a waitress or dancer would pass by.

He stopped fidgeting. I let the table slack and stepped to the side of it, so he couldn't throw it at me, and so I could run to the stairs when it came down to it, or so I was at an angle to punch him when he moved.

Boom. He knocked the table across the aisle and into the rail. Glass flew over the edge. I ran down the steps, pushing a waitress out of my way. She came flying down the stairs behind me. Wally trampled everything in his path. He would break me in a closed space. I ran for room to fight. More ladies got in my way. With demon speed, Wally pushed me through the exit. I fell forward, but tucked my arms and rolled to a standing position in the parking lot. This was it.

I turned to face him. Whoever he was. Huge, shirt untucked, wrinkled, his hair sweaty and sticking to his forehead, his huge hands opening and closing. I stepped backwards slowly. There was a large garbage bin behind me, the parking lot in front of me and the highway to my left. This was as much room as I would get.

I felt the tingle in my chest. It sunk to my feet and weighted them. I force slid them forward. Toward Wally. I couldn't kick him. He was still my principal. If I threw a punch at him, it had to be perfect. I brought my hands up in fists. He growled that he would kick my ass, like his sound was slowed down. And I watched him stumble toward me, a frame at a time. With jumpcuts. As he finally stopped saying he was gonna kick my ass. He still slobbered, spit. Like outside air had made him slower, drunker.

I had to beat him now and on my terms.

"What happened to 'k,' Wally?"

He stopped stumbling and straightened up. Asked "What?" with his face, spine, shoulders, and voice.

"What happened to 'k'?"

"Which bitch is she?"

"It's no bitch. It's the Puerto Rican kid that disappeared from school, you ignorant mutherfucker."

"What the fuck are you talking about?"

"We saw his old man come to school to pick up his shit."

"That kid!" and his body lit up like a light bulb, he seemed lighter even, there standing straight, making sense. "That kid killed himself, Marquez."

All the badassness drained out of me through my heavy feet.

He laughed. "Did you have something to do with that, too?" He threw his head back when he laughed. He flung his arms in the air when he laughed. "Did he call you before he did it?" he shouted at the sky. "Did you ignore him?" he shouted at me. "Or did you think he was joking? Did you think it was a prank?" He stumbled straight at me. Everything slowed down. Everything moved frame by frame, and I missed a few. He'd beaten me academically, mentally. There was only one way left.

He pushed me. I went back, back, back, and slammed against the garbage bin. "Well, he was serious." There weren't any openings for me to aim at. "As serious as a heart attack. And *this* is serious, too."

There was all kinds of space to his left, to the outside where I sidestepped and shouted, "Fuck you, Asshole. If that kid had killed himself we would've heard an announcement. You're full of shit, you shit-faced loser."

He leaned against the big brown bin. "No, Marquez. I didn't announce jackshit because he was no longer a student at our fine institution. He got kicked out for confessing to stealing Biology tests, you piece of shit." He leaned over as if he was about to puke, and shouted at the cement, "How do you make kids listen to you? Do you suck their dicks? Do you let them use your ma?" He spit, wiped his mouth with his suit coat and looked up at me. My tongue tingled, almost numb.

"You saw his old man. That PR probably beat the shit outta him for stealing. He beat him like I should beat you. Like I'm gonna beat you." He got off the bin, straightened out his coat again, then stumbled towards me. But this time I heard the bits of broken glass under his shoes. For the first time I heard it, like someone had just busted a car window and shoved it there. "I never met a murderer before. I never met someone who pushed someone over the edge."

"Fuck you, Old Man." I got my feet back and circled. "If that kid did kill himself, it was you and your school that did it. You and the shit you stuffed down his brain and his Old Man's brain. That did it."

He stopped and pointed his finger at me. "That's your school." He was shaking when he said it. "I got paid to keep it up. I took your money, but I won't take the guilt, punk."

"Listen here, you pervert. You asshole licker. I heard you used to hang around the shower room staring at the naked boys, you faggot. How did you pass the psychological screening to get the job, you homo..."

And then he was on me.

The rest is under water, in bad lighting. All that weight, that mad, angry weight pushing me backwards until I slammed against a parked car. He fell on me, growling. I spit and spit and spit. I catch glimpses of his face, scrunched, in pain. I must be hitting him. There's blood on his mouth. My knuckles hurt. I ripped his shirt at the collar grabbing at him. And slowly, from my arms, he moves his hands to my neck, and his eyes are wide open, his head taking thuds from my fists, and then his fat fingers and his nails slicing into my neck. My throat burning, my Adam's apple about bursting. Salt in my mouth.

A face appeared behind him. There were hands on his face. Hands grabbing his arms. A hand around his eyes. Ripping him off me before I died.

I fell to the cement. I can remember the asphalt coming toward me. It hurt less.

The good Samaritans didn't beat the fuck out of him, just got him off me and tried to keep him still. By then, Wally must've been shook sober. I was standing against the car I'd fallen on and put a dent in. He broke free and my helpers had had enough. They stepped away. Wally stepped away from them. He stopped and looked at me. I wasn't scared. I didn't feel anything. I felt like I was staring at Big Foot. He stopped and looked at me. Just looked at me. And I looked at him. And then he limped off into the parking lot, passing cars until he turned and stepped into a row. He bent down into a car. Pulled away.

The guys asked me if I was okay.

I shook my head. Thanked them for saving my life.

"What the fuck happened?"

"He thought I was having an affair with his wife."

"Holy shit!" "I woulda wrung your neck too!" "Oh, shit, guy."
"The thing is I don't know who the hell his wife is."

A cop car pulled in with its lights flashing, without any sound.

One of my helpers waved over the cops. He appointed himself my representative. The cops stepped out.

"What happened?"

"Some crazy mutherfucker tried to kill me 'cause he thought I was banging his wife."

"Did you know the man?"

"Barely. We started shooting the shit at another bar, and then we decided to come here. He said he knew the joint. He didn't mention anything about strangling me."

"Do you wanna press charges?"

"If it'll do any good."

He stuck his head into the window of the police car and pulled out a clipboard. The other cop sat inside and shut off the siren light. He said some shit into his radio. I couldn't hear, but I wanted to know.

"What's your name?"

"Lorenzo Cassanova..." I had to say that. I was underage, I was about to file police charges. But I knew they would never trace me or Lorenzo. And I thought, too, that it might be better to take care of Wally my own way. Cops at his door. TV cameras waiting for him after he posts bail. A black and white picture of me on the screen, black and white to emphasize the bruises, the marks. No. Better for me to get Wally my own way. Not theirs.

After the cops left, I sat in my car in the parking lot for hours because I had nowhere to go.

I felt like I'd been hurled from a moving train, dropped off in some town, with no money.

I didn't know if it'd been a near-death experience. My life hadn't flashed before my eyes. Maybe I hadn't lived long enough or good enough for that to happen. And even as I watched Big Foot leave, it was still like a dream. Even the choking.

I felt so tired. His fingers lightly on my neck now. His hands still softly pressed against my throat.

All I had was my car. My feet, my ass, my back, all busy with fatigue. My body sending signs to each part to make sure they were all still there. I'd gotten fucked up pretty good. I sat there just thinking about it. Like my dad does, sitting there with his arms crossed, just thinking and rethinking and thinking about shit.

Until the bar closed.

I watched all the customers leave, cabs pulled up, men picked up some of the dancers who came out dressed like regular women, in loose blue jeans shorts, some in sweat pants, all dressed PG-13.

Finally Farah walked out with a duffel bag in her hand, wearing a baggy white T-shirt and not-so-tight blue jeans.

I figured Farah's place was the only place to go. Even if I could've gone to my parent's house, showing up all shit-kicked-out-of would've freaked out my mom. It was best to go some place where I could get some time on my own, could be not cared so much for and allowed to let the poison bleed out. "Hey, Farah. I mean, Genie. Hey, Farah."

She was walking about ten feet in front of my car.

"Sorry, Sweetie, I gotta get going home."

"I'm not Sweetie, it's me..." And I couldn't remember what the fuck she knew me by.

She stuck her hand into a pocket on the side of her duffel bag and tiptoed toward my car. "T-O! Where'd you go? I was ready to mace you." She pulled her hand out of the duffel and moved toward me.

I stuck my head out of the car.

"Oh my God! What happened to you?" I almost get killed and she hadn't even bothered to listen to the gossip about the fight in the parking lot because there was not money involved.

"I'll explain if you give me a ride to your place."

"Sure, Jester's working tonight."

And I froze in opening the door. That was possibly ass-kicking number two.

She opened the door the rest of the way. "Don't worry. Everything'll be fine." She helped me out of the car, leaned me against my car, rolled the window up in my car. "Even if say he does show up, which he shouldn't, I can say you called me for help because you got...What happened to you?"

"My father attacked me." It seemed smart to tell her the truth in a way she'd understand. I figured I might as well live next to nice-and-warm-and-soft for a few minutes, in as least complicated a way as possible. Besides, I didn't have the strength to say, "The guy who licked your ass, yeah, well he kicked my ass. You got the better end of the deal, I must say. At least you got some money out of it."

She drove me to her place.

I dreamed about it. All in slow motion again. And when I woke up Monday morning, I couldn't remember everything that well, but my body had recorded it all and kept playing it back to itself, my knee bitter over the fall to the asphalt.

I slept 'til twelve and just lay in bed, alone.

Farah's bedroom was lit up from the sun again. And again I was fucked up. I could smell coffee and bread. That was nice. Even if the food wasn't for me, I had a few minutes with the smell where it seemed like it was for me. And the bed was soft and the sheets were soft against my skin. I turned and there was an impression where Farah had left the bed bruised, though I could barely remember her in the dream about last night. Except for Wally talking into her ass. "Her ass had gotten my ass kicked," I had to stop thinking.

"You're keeping comedian's hours, T-O," her voice said from behind me. And that meant that Jester had fucked her plenty of times after work and slept till noon. And what she said was a small reminder of who I had wanted to be. Her saying my name reminded me of who I was with her, and the comedian business reminded me of my line of work. And work was what it was. It was all work. I would be working the rest of my life. And then I would die.

She was very talkative at breakfast in her baggy jeans and oversized white sweatshirt. I called her "Sweetie" plenty of times for her effort, whatever it was she'd said. But I could not wait for her to go some place so I could just lay still in her apartment and think about the world rolling over me.

She started asking questions about my father. So I kept lying and telling the truth. I couldn't be anything with her unless I cut all ties with the reality that had led me to the lie I was with her.

Swallowing the egg was hard, even if the bits were small.

"The old man's got a ton of CDs, a few investments here and there, but most of it is in the bank. Kind of his modern day mattress."

"It's not like he earned it. It was all a freak stroke of luck he doesn't want to share with you. We've got to take him for all he's worth," she said about my father. I'd let her know that everything was in both our names and signatures. "This is child abuse," she said, which meant she knew I was full of shit with all my fake ID's, but she knew I was good enough with them for her to never doubt they would always work. "You can sue him broke or rob him blind." And we plotted his murder next, after Jester's, I supposed.

I hoped when my turn came that it would be quick—poison maybe. I hoped she liked me enough to make it quick. She kissed me when I thanked her for the toast, lightly buttered like I loved, I lied to her.

"Are you gonna be able to go to work?" she asked.

And in this world I wore makeup, had a routine to exercise, worked nights, slept days. Practiced and practiced saying the same words I'd conjured over and over again.

"Yeah, Sweetie. I'll be at work tonight. And you?"

"Sure."

Farah walked into the bedroom. I heard her pulling or tugging at blankets, ruffling, then snapping blankets. I heard her hands wiping across the sheets. Her rustling a plastic bag.

I never imagined her doing housework. And if I had, it would have been doing housework naked.

"I put your things in this bag. So you won't lose them." She held up a white garbage bag. Through the thin skin of the bag, my dirty black socks, red underwear, and black T-shirt looked like weird intestines in a stomach she was holding up, dropped on the floor where I would trip on it.

"If you need to take a shower, I put some towels in the bathroom for you. Just leave them in the hamper when you're done." She gave me a quick kiss on the mouth and took away my plate and mug. I think I was done. She washed them right away.

Farah put the clean dishes in a cabinet over the sink. She wiped her hands on her sweatshirt, turned, and looked around the place. "Oh, your shoes." She walked back to the bedroom. She took a little while. Either she checked for something else or she stopped to wipe my fingerprints off something. She was good.

It dawned on me at the moment that it was kind of weird that even though she was Jester's girlfriend there was no sign that he had ever been there. His picture wasn't even on the wall with the pictures of comedians. (She had pictures of David Letterman, Andrew Dice Clay, Jay Leno, Freddy Prince, Eddie Murphy...I guess Jester's picture just didn't fit. And he had no problem with that. He knew that. Or she took it down while he was not here.)

I wondered how many other bodies had been swept under the floorboards.

She had a purse in her hand all of a sudden, one she could probably make appear and disappear. "I'm gonna find out about a Realtors class. I keep thinking about it, so I'm gonna get some facts and see what's up." She kissed what was left of me, left her spit on my lips. I felt it squirm.

It was the first moment I had to myself in a long time. I should've stopped and meditated but I didn't know how. To stop and think and think about nothing. My brain was racing from being watched. From thinking of my next move, second guessing everything around me, looking for motives.

I was sitting in a stripper's living room, barefoot, no shirt on, and no underwear under my pants. I was suppossed to be in Amercian History. The fact that I wasn't, made me feel cool. I could feel the cool rise from my diaphram, like I was flexing, muscle slipping up to my shoulders. Then my neck ached.

I needed a plan beyond school, beyond Farah, beyond my family, and beyond Jester.

And there was a plan that had been unravelling toward me for years, and Farah had put into words. There was some money that had passed from taxpayers' hands to the government's hands to my father's hands who chose not to pass it when it came my turn to hold out my hand. My dad decided to spend it on himself, on his house.

I thought that it was simply a matter of picking the right person to collect what I was due.

Of course creating an all new personality was not only cowardly, but could also be a sign of psychosis, what with me creating a new name, a new person for a specific task, not just letting the person develop. I would be creating him just to fool myself, because of course no one else could find out about him—or all of me would go to jail.

So I had to have the balls to send either Rosendo, Tio, Juan, Arterio or Lorenzo. One of them had to do the job.

From the back of my mind came a voice that said, "I'll do it." I recognized the voice of Marquez, back from the dead. He was used to killing fathers. He simply stepped out of the grave, simply walked to the front and slipped on the black gloves, made the call.

I could be dropped off in any town and work my way to the top—as long as I had a car, a topless-dancer for a girlfriend, and a dad with prize money to steal from. _tragic_

PANDORO'S BOX

It's some kind of gentlemens agreement that I shook on only because I never broke it. I knew that in my mom and dad's bedroom, in the closet where I used to rummage for his Zoot Suiter clothes, he kept his little case, a locked black box sort of thing. And in there he kept his important papers. It had a little padlock, and he kept the key in the top part of the closet where the hats were stored, in the change box. I knew I wasn't supposed to go in there. When we had to go over important papers, he rummaged through the case and brought them to me. He brought them to me to read, to translate the terms for the certificates of deposit, to calculate the possible interest on bank accounts, to list the contents of the safe deposit boxes, and to sign, sign, he would say, so that the bank would know my signature. And then he would hide the papers again.

It was a Monday, so Marquez knew my mom and Rosie's mom would go to the supermarket in the Hernandez-mobile. She would give Mr. "H" a ride to work, and my dad always gave him shit for this. "Deed da leetle lady get joo to work on time, Hernandez? Deed she?"

And Papa.

He always left the house at 8 a.m., as if he were going off some place to work. He made a big spectacle of it. Had breakfast, coffee, read the paper, kissed mom good bye, said bye to me, warmed the car up, and pulled away to go God knows where.

God knows what he did with all that time.

All I had to do was walk inside the house. Through the living room, up the stairs, through the hall, into the bedroom where my mother and father fucked, and in front of the closet. Open the doors. Suitcoat sleeves brush against my face as I leaned in, picked up the black box by the handles, placed it on the bed.

It wasn't a big deal. It was no major break-in to open it. But oh, the things that got out. Adultery, Jealousy, Avarice, Injustice, Racism, flying out in bell-bottom pants, some with glittery wings, white three-piece suits, in a puff of smoke and disco ball lights from some source at the bottom of the black box. But the only thing that could be left at the bottom, the thing that always follows, as either a dirty trick, a consolation prize, or hope, at the bottom is an enormous piece of blank, clean vellum waiting to be written on, curled up at the ends like a scroll waiting to roll, covering the entire bottom. A piece of angel food cake, a piece of angel wing, left there by some angel who knew I would need so much help to fly straight, who knew that someday I would find out that there were no papers from the Illinois Lottery Commission.

Instead, beneath the vellum there are twelve, small, old, tattered-covered books. No titles on the cover, only "Diary." I open one. The letters squirm on the page. Packed close, there are no paragraph breaks, only passages in different colored pencil, different colored pen. All capital letters. I shake my head in shame, guessing that my father's more of an illiterate than I'd thought. Until I read one of the passages.

WE HAD NO INTENTION OF SELLING THE LAND I WAS SUPPOSED TO GET SOME TO GIVE TO MY HUSBAND TO HAVE MY CHILDREN GROW ON TO WORK TO GET CROPS OR WORK TO SURVIVE BUT TO HAVE SOMEPLACE TO KEEP MY ROOTS PLANTED BUT THE MEN FROM THE MOVIES DID NOT CARE DID NOT UNDERSTAND THAT NO IN SPANISH MEANT THE SAME THING IN ENGLISH TO THEM IT MEANT TRY SOMETHING ELSE ASK US A DIFFERENT WAY

It was my grandmother. It was a letter in a bottle from my father's mother.

I'd read and written on the forms. I knew what was on them, how they shaped my father, but these books I never knew existed, did not know what they held, had never touched, read, or written in them. These, not the papers, were what my father did not want me to see. These could hurt him more.

I took the books, a checkbook, a certificate of deposit, and an envelope with cash. I took everything and left him with an empty chest, as if I'd ripped out his heart. I replaced the gorgeous white sheets of long paper that had covered the tattered books. I wasn't sure how much they cost my father, but they were beautiful, shiny white, velvety, even though fibers showed, and curly on the ends. And I wondered what my dad thought he was going to write on those sheets. But I didn't have time to wonder.

I walked through the living room, my arms burdened with my loot. I put the diaries down, walked to the door, opened it and who but who was there but "A." "What the fuck is he doing here?" I thought. And then I said, "What the fuck are you doing here?"

But he wasn't listening to what I asked. He was staring inside the house, leaning against the door frame, and he said, "This is so weird. I could swear I've seen this house before."

"Fuck what you've seen, what the fuck are you doing here?"

"This is how you greet a friend?"

I carefully placed the diaries on the floor then grabbed him by the shirt, getting his skinny tie in my fist, pulled him into the house, slammed the door. "Look, friend," I whispered loudly into his face so the furniture could not hear and repeat, "this is not a good time to drop by for a visit. I really and truly only need or want to know what the fuck you are doing here."

He pulled out of my grip. He looked surprised, mad, like he was about to cry. He stepped out of grabbing range but still within lunging range and deeper into my house. "Well, you asshole, the school sent me to give you your homework and to tell you that they're gonna kick your ass out if you miss any more days."

I'd missed only two days that week, but my earlier attendance abuses apparently had caught up with me.

"Fuck 'em. Marquez can't go to school today. He's feeling very, very ill. He's never felt worse in his life. If he's still alive tomorrow, he'll visit the school, wearing his little black gloves, you tell 'em he got little black gloves on."

"I don't give a fuck if you got BLACK UNDERWEAR on, mutherfucker! I already did better and told 'em about your black garter belt," he raised his arms to emphasize his point, walked in the direction of the door, which I went to and opened for him, "I told them to save their homework, to save their calls—you know they couldn't reach you, no one knew your damn address—I still don't know how the fuck Wally got it..."

"WALLY!" I slammed the door, "That mutherfucker's got this address?" I grabbed him by the shirt again.

He grabbed me back and shook me, "Stop it with the grabbing shit."

I let go of him, not 'cause he was a bad-ass but because he had the information I needed. "Who sent you?"

"Wally fuckin' sent me. But I knew better then to lug your books around with me 'cause I know and I told them too, that you don't need homework, you're gonna be famous, oh so fuckin' famous."

I looked at him and I couldn't tell if he was being a smart ass or a fan. "Fuck you," I told him. "What Wally tell you to tell me?"

"I told you: to get your ass back in school. You got one more day before they kick you out and you don't graduate."

Amazing. That Wally had balls. He went back to work. And then he sent this fuck with either a peace offering or a threat. Maybe the prick was actually looking out for me. Or trying to pay me back. Or offering me a little bribe, which I could use. "Tell them you got here, conveyed your message and then left."

He walked out with his head down, like he'd been turned down for an autograph or betrayed by a friend. As nice as I could be to him, in that situation at that second, was not to tell him, "You're gonna be really good at conveying important messages for important people. Someday you're gonna be a big, big, man," which I correctly prophesied.

I didn't know what else to do but close the door behind him, stretch my will to wait two minutes to let him leave.

All I wanted to do was read the diaries.

And I had to get out of there before my mom, Mrs. Hernandez, or—God forbid—my father! got home, before a squad car passed by, before I came to one of my senses and shouted "For God's sake, get out! I'm robbing my father today. I'll go to school fucking tomorrow!"

It was easy to find a place where no one knew me, the right place to park and read my diaries. Finding a place where you belong. That's the hard part.

As Much
of The Very
Personal Diary
As I Can Share

I AM NOT NOTICED OFTEN IF I AM THEY THINK I AM
AN EXTRA THERE ARE NOT MANY MEXICANS HERE THEY
JUST DON'T SEE ME IF THEY DO THEY THINK I AM ABOUT
TO CLEAN THEY WOULD ONLY NOTICE A BIG STAR EITHER
I AM INVISIBLE OR I HAVE TO BE A BIG STAR I LIKE IT
BECAUSE I CAN GO ANYWHERE I WANT I SLEEP ON THE SETS
I PUT ON THE COSTUMES I HAVE BEEN IN SOME MOVIES I
MAKE MONEY BY PRETENDING I WORK PLACES I KNOW
HOW TO WORK THE DRY CLEANERS ON THE LOT ONE OF
THE MANAGERS THINKS I WORK THERE THE OTHER DAY
HE SAW ME ON THE LOT AND SAID I NEEDED TO WORK
THE WEEKEND I SHOOK MY HEAD AND KEPT WALKING I
SUPPOSE I SHOULD SHOW UP SATURDAY I WOULD HATE
TO LOSE MY JOB

THEY KNOW WHO I AM BUT BECAUSE I WAS BORN ON
THIS LAND BECAUSE MY UMBILICAL CORD IS BURIED HERE
THEY HAVE PAINTED A SIGN OVER MY HEAD THE WAY THEY
DO TO ACTRESSES ON THE WAY IN OR THE WAY OUT SO I
AM NOT TO BE TOUCHED HE SAYS I CAN STAY HERE AS
LONG AS I WANT

HE MEANS I CAN HAUNT THE PLACE I HEAR THE CREW
MEMBER CALL ME THE MEXICAN GHOST THE ONES WHO
KNOW MEXICANS CALL ME LA LLORONA

HE IS THE BOSS OF ALL OF THIS HE TELLS EVERYONE
WHAT TO DO AND EVEN WHEN HE ISNT AROUND EVERY-
THING IS FOLLOWING HIS ORDERS THATS WHAT HE DOES
HE PUTS EVERYTHING IN ORDER HE WORKS AND WORKS
AND WORKS

HE COMES TO ME HE KNOWS WHAT MY PARENTS LOST
FOR THIS PLACE TO BEGIN

IF HE KNOWS WHO I AM THAT MEANS EVERYONE
KNOWS WHO I AM THEY TREAT ME THE WAY HE TELLS
THEM TO TREAT ME HE TELLS THEM HOW TO DO EVERY-
THING HOW TO MOVE THE CAMERAS HOW TO HANG THE
COSTUMES WHERE TO PUT THE LADDERS HE CAN TELL
WHERE I AM BY THE THINGS THAT IVE MOVED I LEAVE
HIM MESSAGES BY HIDING A PRETEND TREE OR LEAVING
OUT A PRINCESS'S SHOE

EVERYTIME HE SEES ME HE SAYS ONE EXTRA WORD TO
ME AT FIRST HE JUST SHOOK HIS HEAD THEN HE WAVED
AND THEN HE LOOKED RIGHT INTO MY EYES AND I SMILED
AND MADE HIM SMILE AND I DONT WANT TO SAY HOW
HANDSOME HE IS BECAUSE HE IS THE ONE WHO HELPED
THE MOVIE STUDIO TAKE MY PARENTS FARM EVEN IF HE
WAS NOT THERE WHEN THEY SIGNED HE IS HERE NOW
AND ITS BECAUSE OF HIM THAT THE PLACE DOES NOT
FALL APART

HE IS SO YOUNG MAYBE ONLY A LITTLE OLDER THAN I
AM YOUNGER THAN MOST OF THE BEAUTIFUL ACTRESSES
ON THE LOT HE DOESNT JOKE LIKE THE WORKERS HE

COMES IN AND THE WHOLE PLACE STOPS WHAT ITS DO-
ING TO SEE IF HE WILL TELL THEM HOW TO DO IT RIGHT
AND HE WALKS IN AND CAN TELL WHAT NEEDS TO BE
FIXED OR TAKEN AWAY AND WHO CAN TAKE OVER AND
THEN HE JOKES AND EVERYONE LAUGHS AT ANYTHING
DIFFERENT HE MIGHT SAY

EVERYONE LOVES HIM

TODAY HE ASKED ME IF I WAS THE ONE WHO MOVED
THE SCARECROWS FROM THE SET TO THE PARKING LOT I
DID NOT LIE AND I CAN STILL FEEL MY FACE SMILING AT
HOW NICE HE WAS TALKING TO ME AND I THINK I REMEM-
BER HIM TALKING TO ME BEFORE THAT

I DO NOT KNOW WHY THEY PICKED OUR FARM I
THOUGHT THEY WERE FOOLISH TO EVEN TRY TO BUY
OUR FARM TO GROW ANYTHING ON BUT THAT IS NOT
WHAT THEY WANTED THEY WANTED TO POUR CEMENT
OVER EVERYTHING AND FILM MOVIES ON THE LAND AND
I DO NOT KNOW WHY THEY PICKED OUR SPOT AND THEY
NEVER SAID WHY BUT THEY SAID THAT THEY REALLY RE-
ALLY WANTED THE LAND AND WE SHOULD SELL IT TO
THEM AND THAT THEY WOULD GIVE MY FATHER A LOT
OF MONEY

WE HAD NO INTENTION OF SELLING THE LAND I WAS
SUPPOSED TO GET IT TO GIVE TO MY HUSBAND TO HAVE
MY CHILDREN GROW ON TO WORK TO GET CROPS OR
WORK TO SURVIVE BUT TO HAVE SOMEPLACE TO KEEP MY
ROOTS PLANTED BUT THE MEN FROM THE MOVIES DID
NOT CARE DID NOT UNDERSTAND THAT NO IN SPANISH
MEANT THE SAME THING IN ENGLISH TO THEM IT MEANT
TRY SOMETHING ELSE ASK US A DIFFERENT WAY

THE MONEY COULD NEVER BE ENOUGH THEY COULDNT
PAY FOR THE BABIES I DID NOT HAVE YET THE HUSBAND
I HAD NOT MET

SO THEY SAID THAT THEY COULD PROVE THAT WE DID
NOT OWN THE LAND THAT THE SPANISH DEED THAT SAID
MY FATHERS FATHER OWNED THE LAND WAS NOT GOOD

BECAUSE THE SPANISH HAD LOST MANY WARS AND THEN
THEY SAID THAT WE WOULD HAVE TO GO BACK TO
MEXICO IF THEY WENT TO THE GOVERNMENT WITH THIS
PROBLEM BUT MY FATHER DID NOT UNDERSTAND BECAUSE
OUR FAMILY HAD NEVER LEFT MEXICO BECAUSE MEXICO
HAD LEFT OUR FAMILY IT WAS UP TO MEXICO TO COME
BACK TO US HE SAID BECAUSE WE HAD NEVER LEFT THE
LAND

BUT THE PICTURE PEOPLE HAD ALREADY DECIDED
EVEN BEFORE THEY ASKED US THEY HAD STARTED BUILD-
ING BUILDINGS VERY CLOSE BY HAD SENT TRUCKS AND
MEN AND HORSES

WHEN SOME OF THE FIRST BUILDINGS WERE UP SOME-
TIMES A PICTURE MAN WOULD COME TO OUR HOUSE IN A
CAR FOLLOWED BY DOZENS OF COWBOYS AND INDIANS
SHOOTING THEIR GUNS AND HOLLERING

OF COURSE WE DIDNT ANSWER AT FIRST AND THEN
THEY WOULD RUN AROUND THE HOUSE ON THE HORSES
AND THEN LEAVE BUT I NOTICED THAT THEY ALL GOT
ALONG FINE AND JOKED AND TALKED TOGETHER AND
WOULD SHOOT EACH OTHER OVER AND OVER AGAIN
WITHOUT DYING

IT GOT TO WHERE WE WOULD SIT OUTSIDE EVERY DAY
AND WATCH FOR WHO THEY WOULD SEND AND LAUGH
AT THE KNIGHTS OR THE ANIMALS AND THE GANGSTERS
WOULD WHISTLE AT ME AND ASK ME MY NAME AND MY
FATHER WOULD SHOUT NO NO NO AT THEM HE EVEN
PAINTED IT ON A SIGN AND HUNG IT IN THE FRONT WIN-
DOW

BUT THEY WOULD NOT STOP AND MORE BUILDING
WENT UP CLOSER TO OUR HOUSE AND WE COULD NOT
GET ANY WORK DONE OR GET ANYONE TO HELP US TRY
TO GROW ANYTHING AND THE MEN WHO CAME CAME
ALONE NOW AND TALKED MORE ABOUT THE GOVERNMENT
AND OFFERED JUST A LITTLE MORE MONEY AND MADE
PROMISES ABOUT US BEING ABLE TO STAY NEAR BY AND
MY FATHER JUST GOT TIRED

AFTER MY DAD SIGNED THE PAPERS WAS THE FIRST TIME ONE OF THEM TRIED TO KISS ME

AFTER I HAD WALKED IN THE GERMAN VILLAGE AND VISITED THE JUNGLE THEY MADE AND SAW THE STREETS OF NEW YORK WAS WHEN I LET THE HANDSOMEST MAN WHO TRIED TO KISS ME KISS ME

MAYBE THESE MEN WILL NOT LIE THEY SAY THEY ARE IN A REVOLUTION OF FILM BUT THERE ARE NO GUNS SO I THINK IT WILL GO GOOD AT LEAST THEY MIGHT DO WHAT THEY PROMISE

IF YOU DONT KNOW SOMEONE AND MEET HIM FOR THE FIRST TIME AND HE IS A WITH A YOUNG PRETTY GIRL YOU NEVER KNOW IF IT IS HIS WIFE DAUGHTER GIRL-FRIEND MISTRESS OR ONE OF HIS DAUGHTERS FRIENDS EXCEPT IF ITS ME IF IM NOT CARRYING A TRAY IF IM SO PRETTY OF COURSE IM NOT A DAUGHTER OF COURSE IM NOT HIS WIFE SOMEONE LIKE ME IS NEVER A GIRLFRIEND SO THEY KNOW WHAT I AM AND THEY WANT ME TO BE THEIRS TOO NOT JUST BECAUSE THEY LIKE ME OR THINK IM BEAUTIFUL BUT YOU HAVE TO BE BEAUTIFUL BECAUSE THEY ALL KNOW WHAT I AM AND WHOEVER THEY MEET WHEN I AM WITH HIM WILL KNOW WHAT I AM

I GET TO BE AN ACTRESS SOMETIMES I PUT ON THE COSTUMES AND WALK AROUND LIKE THE EXTRAS DO OR I PRETEND TO CLEAN OR I PICK UP A PAD OF PAPER AS IF IM DELIVERING IT IF IM STOPPED I PRETEND I DONT SPEAK ENGLISH ONE TIME A DIRECTOR STOPPED AND WANTED TO KNOW WHO I WAS AND WHAT I WAS DOING ON HIS LOT I PRETENDED NOT TO KNOW WHAT HE WAS SAYING THEN A GUARD CAME BY AND WHISPERED IN HIS EAR HIS EYES OPENED AND THEN HE LEFT I LIKE TO PRETEND HE TOLD HIM THAT I WAS HIS HIS I MEAN HIM HIM HIS WOMAN

I THINK MY DAD THOUGHT THAT ONCE WE SOLD WE COULD REST THAT THEY WOULD LEAVE US ALONE THEN THAT IS NOT THE WAY IT WORKS WE COULD NEVER REST AGAIN I WOULD NEVER REST AGAIN AND MY CHILDREN WILL NEVER REST LIFE IS WORK AND THE WORK WILL NOT

END UNTIL YOU DIE NO THATS NOT RIGHT THE TRUTH IS THAT MY LIFE IS WORK I WILL WORK UNTIL I DIE AND THEN MY CHILDREN WILL WORK UNTIL THEY DIE AND WE WILL WORK TO KEEP FROM DYING SOMETIMES I KNOW WHY SOMETIMES I AM NOT AFRAID TO DIE

WE TOOK THE MONEY AND THEY TOOK THE LAND AND SAID WE COULD STILL LIVE ON IT BUT OF COURSE WE COULD NOT FARM AND MY DAD DID NOT KNOW WHAT ELSE TO DO AND WE HAD NO WHERE TO GO AND THE BUILDINGS KEPT GETTING CLOSER AND THE ACTORS KEPT COMING BY THE ONLY THING THAT CHANGED WAS THAT MY DAD HAD TO TAKE HIS SIGN DOWN AND COULD NOT KEEP TELLING THEM NO HE COULD NOT TELL THEM ANY-THING AND EVEN IF HE DID THEY WOULD NOT HEAR BECAUSE HE DIDNT EXIST ANYMORE OUR LITTLE HOUSE WAS JUST A SET WAITING FOR A MOVIE THAT WOULD NEVER BE MADE

STARH IS JEWISH I CALL HIM THE STAHR OF DAVID MY FATHER HATES STAHR HE HATES ALL THE BOSSES HE THINKS ALL THE BOSSES ARE JEWISH MY FATHER SAYS HE HATES THE JEWS REALLY HE HATES THE BOSSES I TRY TO TELL HIM

THE BOSSES THEY DONT HATE MEXICANS IM SURE THEY HARDLY EVEN THINK OF THEM

I DONT KNOW WHY IT HAPPENED TODAY BUT IT DID I DONT KNOW HOW IT REALLY HAPPENED BUT I HAVE A VISION IN IT IN MY HEAD WHICH IS A LOT DIFFERENT THAN THE WAY I IMAGINED IT WHICH IS DIFFERENT THAN THE WAY I REMEMBER IT BUT IT WAS WONDERFUL HE ASKED ME TO HIS OFFICE FOR LUNCH THAT MAGICAL MEAL I HEAR EVERYONE INVITING EVERYONE ELSE TO THEY INVITE EACH OTHER TO LUNCH IN FRONT OF ME AS IF I COULDNT UNDERSTAND THE WORD AFTER HEARING TWICE THE WAY ITS USED AS IF I DONT EAT THEY INVITE EACH OTHER TO LUNCH IN FRONT OF ME BECAUSE I AM NOT THERE BUT HE ASKED ME TO LUNCH AND WE ATE AMERI-CANS EAT DIFFERENTLY THAN MEXICANS HE EATS LIKE PEOPLE IN THE MOVIES WHICH IS PROBABLY WHY THE

PEOPLE IN THE MOVIES EAT THE WAY THEY DO HE TELLS THE ACTORS HOW TO EAT WHEN THEY EAT WITH HIM THEY WATCH HIM THE WAY I WATCHED HIM AND THEY GO ON AND EAT LIKE THAT IN FRONT OF OTHERS WHO WATCH THEM THEY USE DISHES FOR EVERYTHING THE FOOD IS SMALL THIN AND SWEET AND SERVED A LITTLE AT A TIME JUST ENOUGH FOR THE MOMENT AND THEN RIGHT BEFORE YOU FINISH HERE COMES MORE I LOVE LUNCH

IT HAS BEEN A LONG TIME SINCE I HAVE BEEN ABLE TO SIT STILL LONG ENOUGH TO WRITE MY FATHER KNOWS THIS WORLD HAS TURNED UPSIDE DOWN AGAIN HE SENSES IT I GIVE OFF VIBRATIONS I KNOW I DONT SHOW YET I DONT KNOW HOW HE CAN KNOW BUT HE CAN TELL AND THEN HE YELLS AND THEN HE LOCKS ME IN THE HOUSE AND HOPES THAT WHAT HAS HAPPENED DOES NOT HAP-PEN

THE BABY INSIDE ME WILL LEAD A VERY DIFFICULT LIFE

IT HAS BEEN A LONG TIME SINCE I HAD SOME PLACE TO SIT AND WRITE I TRIED TO WRITE IN ONE OF THE MOVIE LOTS BUT THE SIGHT OF A PREGNANT MEXICAN WOMAN WRITING IS TOO AMAZING FOR THE MOVIE PEOPLE I DOnT WANT STARS STARING AT ME LIKE THAT OTHERWISE THEY CAST GLANCES AT ME TAKE PEEKS AND TRY TO GUESS WHO MADE ME THIS WAY THEY KNOW ITS ONE OF THEM BE-CAUSE I AM BEAUTIFUL AND THEY LET ME STAY ON THE LOT TO BUMP INTO THINGS

AND THE FATHER COULD BE STAHR OR MORETTI OR OLIVIER OR GOMEZ

THE FATHER OF MY CHILD IS THE MOVIE STUDIO AND MY BABY LIES IN THE DARK WAITING FOR THE LIGHT

AND I AM ALONE

I HAD TO SEE HIM ONE LAST TIME BEFORE I KILLED MYSELF BUT IT WASNT LIKE IN THE MOVIES I DID NOT WANT TO SEE HIM TO LET HIM KNOW I LOVED HIM OR TO

TELL HIM I DIDNT LOVE HIM OR TO TRY AND HURT HIM I
WANTED TO LET HIM KNOW THAT I KNEW HOW MUCH MY
FATHERS LAND HAD BEEN WORTH THAT I KNEW THAT HE
HAD ROBBED HIM THAT I HAD HELPED HIM BY PLANTING
IDEAS IN MY FATHERS HEAD THAT MY FATHER COULD BE
AS STUBBORN AS THE LAND ITSELF IF IT HAD NOT BEEN
FOR MY DROP OF A SUGGESTION MY LITTLE IDEA RE-
PEATED AGAIN AND AGAIN AND AGAIN AND AGAIN IF IT
WASNT FOR MY REPEATING HE WOULD HAVE NEVER GAVE
IN HE WOULD BE A HOLE IN THE UNIVERSE A BLIGHT IN
YOUR LAND I KNOW HOW MUCH THE LAND WAS WORTH
TO YOU AND I WANT YOU TO KNOW THAT I TOO KNEW
YOUR COMPANY STOLE THE LAND AND EVEN THOUGH IT
WAS NOT YOU WHO SIGNED THE DEAL IT IS YOU WHO
KEEPS THIS MONSTER ALIVE AND GROWING AND THEN I
LEFT AND I BEGAN TO WALK AND I WILL KEEP WALKING
UNTIL MY NAME HAS EVAPORATED UNTIL MY MEMORY HAS
FADED UNTIL I SEE THE LAND WHERE I AM SUPPOSED TO
RESETTLE AND BEGIN AGAIN I AM GOING TO KILL THE
PERSON I ONCE WAS

AND I WANTED HIM TO KNOW THAT THE CHILD I HAD
IN ME MIGHT NOT BE HIS

HE TOLD ME THAT SOMEDAY HE WOULD PAY ME BACK

That was my father's winning lottery ticket.

ALL EDUCATED WITH NO PLACE TO GO

I thought I was a hyphenated American because I chose to call myself a Mexican-American. But looking over my résumé, I realize I earned this designation because I've worked as a free-lance journalist, teaching-assistant, assistant-editor, and stand-up comedian.

That's why I'm on un-employment.

Always a bridesmaid, never an executive. That's my story. Employers don't want to pay me to be an editor, a professor, a headliner, or a president because they think I'm too easy to hire. I've been around. But really, I'm trying to settle down.

Back during that naïve spring quarter before I finished graduate school, my fianceé was anxious to set a wedding date.

"How about a year after I've been working full-time," I said. I thought I could use the 52 weeks to get adjusted to my new job, make sure our grad-school chums and my work chums got along, get my finances straight, play the lottery.

Well, the fall quarter has just ended. I've got three unemployment checks left, and I'm hassling her to come with me to the justice of the peace so I can be covered by her university plan. (She's a teaching-assistant and has a year and a half left with that hyphen.) Slowly but surely, she's warming to the idea.

Since I earned the degree in May, all I've been able to do with my master of fine arts is visit museums and say, "Yes, that art's fine. That's fine too." And I still have to show people my degree for them to believe me. Earning just a bachelor's degree might've meant I'd be a bachelor forever.

We wanted to have the wedding out here in California, but some of my relatives in Chicago were wary of visiting since Proposition 187 passed. I told them not to worry. As long as they mispronounced the Spanish names of towns they'd be just fine. "San-Joe-Say," I told them to practice. "Sand-Lewis-Abyss-Po."

My parents are very supportive (grocery money when we really need it), but I can see the desperation in their eyes even though they try to hide it behind their tears. "All those diplomas," my poor *mamasita* cries in Spanish, "Kindergarten, eighth grade, high school, regular college, graduate school and still, still you're not married."

I've had three graduations more than anyone else in my family, but I'm also the only one to have three part-time jobs that don't add up to 40 hours a week. I'm an intellectual migrant worker.

When I was still in grad school, folks told me I wouldn't have a problem finding a job; I'd not only have a master's degree, but I spoke Spanish, too.

So far, being bilingual has meant only that I can read the back of the unemployment insurance claim form as well as the front. And to the folks at all those cocktail parties who told me it was a "hot time to be Latino," I must admit that it seems as if our Nielsen ratings are suffering.

But I'm keeping the faith. Instead of scrambling for 25 job leads next week, I'm going to hustle 50. Instead of working 5 free open mikes, I'll suffer 6. Instead of six hours of sleep, I'll settle for five. (That's still a luxury. My dad says he never slept until he turned 30.)

I know that soon I'll come across my dream employer's want ad for the position I perfectly satisfy. She'll write: "Looking for a humorous writer who can handle day after day of exciting challenges and irregular hours, high pay and a thrilling environment. Unpublished preferred. Who wants this post?"

If only she'd give me a ring, I'd shout, "I do! I do!"

What it trickles down to is that some guys are married to their jobs.

I'm just trying to get a commitment.

CODA TO THE DIARY

And my grandfather could be Starh, or Morretti, or Gomez. And my father is the bastard son of Hollywood. A bad case of sombrero hysteria from that rotten sperm, so good at playing the *peladito* because he was born into it. He was the lost generation. Close enough to *the act* that he could feel the shame warm on his skin, but just far enough away that he would not know what it was like to walk across all his lands. Hearing only of past greatness and trapped with a son he could not decipher. Born, destined to don The Hat, the sombrero of hysteria.

And I imagine a private eye sifting his way through California, Arizona, New Mexico, Colorado, Chicago trying and trying to track Gram, to find her on a day she didn't work, to get her to answer the door so he could hand her the handful of dirt so many hands had clung tenaciously to. Only to find her plain, simple, barely marked grave, covered with weeds, with dirt thick on the plaque bearing the name she died with.

And then handing the money to my father, like a birthday card the post office fucked up mailing: a generation too late, crumbled, post office graffiti all over the face instead of apologies.

And somewhere, someone had written a certain paragraph on a certain piece of paper in response to a ghost visiting him Christmas Eve, or voices visiting him after a long, vicious buzz, or a long lost hard-on.

Perhaps it was left in one of their wills. Maybe it was fought over in court. IT finally was settled, and my grandmother was entitled to some money. Guilt money. (It is ALL guilt money, brother.) And WE finally got back a parcel of land that was supposed to be hers.

Maybe grandpa was a good guy.

And his dad was, too.

All of them had their role in forming...

I have learned not to spit in people's mouths.

In disputes over captives, I am unfair in favor of the captive.

My mission as a teacher is to make myself obsolete.

The most infinite journey is startled by the very first step.

From eagles and jaguars, I create men and women.

In the neo-ultraviolet, I can see our hyper-denominators.

The Aztec Love God

Monday Night
or
The Monkey's Paw

There was a Monday-night-sized crowd in one of the few night clubs stubborn enough to open on a Monday night. I got in without Lorenzo.

There were enough people to have a softball game, if we shared pitchers. I had more guests at my Communion party, back when I had friends.

Still, there was a pocket of men staring at the four couples and the four women dancing on the dance floor. The guys pointed with their heads at the best-looking women and grinned at each other. This meant, "Her, that's who I'd talk to if I had the balls, if I get drunk enough."

And I thought that the only reason I didn't talk to the ladies was because I was too busy thinking. But that wasn't true. It dawned on me that I didn't know how to dance. Sure, on a crowded floor, with a few drinks in me, I could act as if I danced so good that I was dancing slightly bad on purpose. But in a wide open room, with the only women in the place and the cowardly lions watching, I couldn't dance for shit.

And I would've liked to have not wanted to. Dancing might have gotten me out of my funk, but I'm a comedian, so I don't want anyone to laugh at me.

The women on the dance floor didn't notice us. Or at least acted as if they were the only people in this huge room with a wet bar where they were blasting the stereo. There were about six women dancing together. And they looked gorgeous, mostly because they didn't notice us, and they dressed up by dressing down, bare shoulders, medium length skirts hanging off the curve of their butts, their hair between fixed-for-work and fired-up-for partying.

Some of them had their shoes off and were teaching each other new steps. They laughed at each other and slapped each other five and patted each other's back and shared tastes of different colored drinks and then danced all in step to a popular tune, one you've heard on your way to work, the one you've stayed in your car just a little longer to finish listening to.

Somewhere in an apartment in a Chicago neighborhood, or maybe one of the suburbs, there was a roomful of girls in small shorts, nighties, underwear even, albums and album jackets on the floor, an old turntable spinning, scratching out their high school songs, girls teaching each other old steps and making up new ones. I wished I could kiss one of them. I wished one of them was my girlfriend. I wished one of them was planning to call me to tell me we couldn't go out tonight but tomorrow—tomorrow—we were on for tomorrow. I wished I could have been a good boyfriend to Rosie, to any one. I wished I could be good.

I'm no idiot. And if I am, it's not 'cause I couldn't tell what was going on. It all reminded me of that story I think everyone, by law, had to read in high school: "The Monkey's Paw," which inspired a few "Twilight Zone" episodes as well as lots of jokes about incompetent or deaf genies screwin' up your order.

So the joke is that I got my three wishes: to be a REAL comedian, to screw sexy women, to blackmail Wally Autruck. But of course each wish was granted with a little twist, and in the end I got fucked.

But fucked up gloriously.

I mean, this was no ordinary fucked up situation that I could've ordinarily fucked myself into.

And the night I rocked Side Splitters was the night I let the genie out of the bottle.

If I had not rocked Side Splitters, I would not have fucked Farah. If I hadn't been drooling over or hadn't gotten together with Farah, I would not have driven Rosie crazy. If I was busy keeping Rosie and myself sane, I wouldn't have gotten kicked out of my house then been at the topless club on Sunday and seen Wally acting lascivious. If I didn't try to blackmail Wally, he would not have beat the shit out of me. If I hadn't gotten my ass kicked, I would not have tried to steal from my father. But then I would never have found out my past. So even the twists on my wishes had twists. If these things had not taken place, I would never have broken the gentlemens agreement with all those gentlemen and looked in my father's black box. The night before, I would have been in bed with millions of other high-school kids on a Sunday night, flipping through TV channels, dreading the prospect of school the next day, counting the hours until I was supposed to wake up to drag my ass to school. Which, of course, was what I didn't want in the first place. I wanted to be a one-in-a-million kid. And so this was the price.

But to simply wish for a boring version of my life was too simple for me. I wanted to be the one-in-a-billion person who kicks his genie's ass. What good was it to get this far, which was really just the beginning, what good was it to get this far into Aztec Love God-ness only to decide that it's nice to just be ordinary, that my life was better when it was simpler? That's what happens in a half-hour sitcom, the short story about the monkey's paw, the joke about the guy who winds up with a ten-inch pianist.

No. Even if I got one foot in the door and the other in my mouth, at least I got an "in." And if I could "make it" on my terms, well, that would be the biggest joke of all. That would be the joke on everyone else who was selling out at every turn, lying, cheating, stealing, and fucking just to get to the next level of lying, cheating, stealing and fucking; or clinging to old safe thoughts that lead to the stereotypes others perceive—sombrero hysteria, or strangled by what is supposed to extol you—sombrero hysteria.

The first step was to come clean. With everyone. About everything. And that would be the biggest joke of it all because it would be truth. And the truth is the funniest thing on earth. People are so unaccustomed to hearing it that it slightly shocks when it's revealed.

A truth. My version. And that was my power. To sift through the static and white noise of everday life and to find and shape a clump of truth. To take the truth and dress it in words.

That was the big lesson. To harness the truth. But I was going for the easy stuff, dressing the women in mens clothes and the men in womens clothes, slapping pink neon serapes on Mexicans in plaid sombreros. I had to make my job a lot harder than that.

The first step was to tell my dad the truth. Then Rosie. "k." Wally. Farah, Jester, Lorenzo.

My father and I will be closer after this. There's no way we couldn't. Me telling him that I had stolen his dark secrets and by making them mine had made them less dark, that could only be good.

Wally, well, let's just say I knew I'd joined his club, like it or not, and I would graduate, absences or not, though I planned to finish my final assignments. I planned to actually do my last tasks in high school.

And my mom, I knew her better. I thought I realized just what a struggle she must go through to be my dad's silent partner. And this made me appreciate and love Rosie more. And it would be hard to tell her what a fiend I had been, but I would have to share that ugly truth with her so that I could be alone, but not sorry, for a while at least.

And my grandmother had been transmitting me messages all along, influencing my gravity, my humor. And I had listened to what I could not filter out, to what transcended the channels that limited my perception. She was the vibration in the air when the right chord was caught. All the frequencies that I was rewarded for not ignoring. She gave me 20 jokes a day like daily diary entries. She gave me a truth beyond the letters and words that sentenced me to a certain reality.

And once I had practiced telling the truth, maybe I could tell a roomful of strangers with booze in front of them, in the dark, maybe with practice I could tell a dark room full of strangers the truth.

✦

The subplots in my life bleed into the main narrative with no seeming direction until I muster the energy to impose one on myself. But even then I can't make all the strands come together in a half hour or a full lifetime.

I stop the car in front of the Cleaver's tomb. There are several cars in front: my mother's car, the Hernandez mobile, a dark blue LTD—an unmarked police squad. I must have been messier than I thought. Wally must have got worried about me, Jester must have wanted to find out if I was sleeping with Farah, Farah must have come looking for me, "k's" father might be in there. Or maybe Rosie's family and my family and a friend decided to have dinner. They invited a guest to fill the empty seat at the table.

I keep driving. A giddiness washes over me like a buzz. I feel like the car should keep moving like I must. I suspect this could be the part where I walk away, make a clean break, improvise plan B, drive west toward Hollywood where legend has it my house came from. And when the gravel you must grovel on is only a few feet away, and you know you don't really have to stoop, it is very hard to grovel.

I can go back to my television home to see how ma and pa are doing, find the people whose image we are made in. This could be the part where I make it big. And I want to be a tough guy as I drive, turn right, drive, turn right again. But it's kind of sad. To have to pussy out. To realize what you've believed in is really a myth. To give up all the parts of you created, fueled, sustained by the myth, and embrace the person you really are, embrace that person and weigh him down so that you are heavier walking, so that you will have to crawl, to do what you think is pussying out, to pussy out again, and again, and again. And the worst part is that they've all done it.

And we'll all do it again, and again, and again. I guess all we're looking for is a little something to make us forget.

I make the last right turn, stop my car in the middle of the street, leave the keys in the ignition, leave the car running, and I walk to the door.

I'm sweating like I'm boiling something inside. Sweat burning my eyes, hominy somewhere deep inside of me. And I stand in front of the door, pausing before I'm devoured, eaten bit by bit, swallowed whole. I transmit myself to my receivers.

And there are strangers in the house, perhaps authorities, plain-clothes cops, maybe the FBI. And they are not hard to believe, so hard as it is to believe that my dad is acting the way that he is acting in front of these strangers.

My father is running from one side of the living room to the other, running in a way people do not run, his legs coming up too high, his knees coming up at right angles, this causing him to almost jump and hop instead of really run from one part of the house to the other. He pumps his arms back and forth with each hop, and these too he pumps at right angles, his arms exactly bent at right angles to his elbow. And he is shouting, and there are people in the house, some of whom I should recognize, others whom I will never know, some of whom are the law, and they have been ignoring his running and shouting which he invigorates with my heavy presence.

And he is shouting, "We have been robbed, son. We have been robbed."

I grab him by the arms, and I stop him from flight, and I look him in the eye and I say, "No, Dad. We have not been robbed."